PRIDE, PREJUDICE, AND THE ALIEN PRINCE

Jove Chambers

Valerie Lennox

Punk Rawk Books

PRIDE, PREJUDICE, AND THE ALIEN PRINCE
© 2022 by Jove Chambers
www.vjchambers.com

Punk Rawk Books

All characters appearing in this work are fictitious. Any resemblance to real persons, living or dead, is purely coincidental.

All rights reserved. No part of this book may be used or reproduced in any manner whatsoever without written permission except in the case of brief quotations embodied in critical articles and reviews.

ISBN: 9798444443200
PRINTED IN THE UNITED STATES OF AMERICA

10 9 8 7 6 5 4 3 2 1

PRIDE, PREJUDICE, AND THE ALIEN PRINCE

Jove Chambers

Valerie Lennox

ONE

elizabeth

Star Trek had it right.

When I was a kid, I used to watch episodes of that show, and I would laugh with the other foster kids in the house about how it was ridiculous to think that all the aliens in the universe looked just like humans only different colors or with little ridges on their foreheads?

But.

Turned out?

Pretty much, yeah. All of the aliens I'd seen since being abducted looked essentially humanoid. No hair, admittedly, none at all. And their skin color ran the gamut of the colors of the rainbow, from bright, bright yellow to deep, dark purple.

Once, since being abducted, however long ago it had been? Days? A week? We'd slept at least six times, but there was no way to measure time out here, and out of the windows all we could see was the expanse of black space, dotted with stars, as far as the eye could see.

Anyway, once, I'd said to Jane that maybe I hadn't been abducted at all, and this was just a psychotic break, and that I had dreamed it all up, because, really, why did the aliens look like *Star Trek* aliens?

She told me that if that were true then she was also having a psychotic break, and how could we both be hallucinating the same things?

Anyway, *these* aliens — the ones standing in front of us now — were different.

Not a lot different, however.

They were all blue. Deep blue, though their skin shimmered a bit green where the light touched them. They had hair. All of them had long, dark hair. One had it gathered into a ponytail at the nape of his neck, but the other two had theirs long and hanging around their faces and down their backs. They had strange hands — not like humans, sort of V-shaped, with three digits on one side and three digits on the other. In the middle, they resembled the Vulcan salute.

If it was a hallucination, it was heavily influenced by *Star Trek*, which I had been a fan of, I had to admit. But more recently, I'd seen *Star Wars* at the theater, and I had yet to see Darth Vader stroll through the halls, and he'd made more of an impression on my psyche, I thought, especially with the creepy breathing.

These aliens had dark hair growing on the back of their hands, but they weren't anywhere near as furry as Chewbacca, and overall, they looked humanoid too. Why *was* that?

"What are they?" one of the blue men said, the one with the ponytail.

I could understand them, not because they were speaking English, but because the rainbow-colored, bald aliens had jammed a squirming black thing in my ear that had wormed little strands inside my flesh and had somehow given me the ability to understand their language.

It wasn't so much a translation as it was that I just *knew* what they meant. It was an odd sensation.

"Humans," said one of the other men, the tallest of

them. "They must have taken them back through the wormhole. I suppose it makes sense. We have long known they'd be compatible with most species in our galaxy."

"It's a violation of the Intergalactic Treatises on Noninterference," said the third.

"Yes," said Tall Blue dryly. "I'm sure smugglers like this care about following the letter of the law."

"If the galactic senate gets wind of it—"

"I doubt anything will happen," said Tall Blue. "The Toth control the senate now, and this has the stink of the Toth all over it."

At this point, Lydia scooted up close to me. We were all—all four of us—stuck in a small room that had a sort of toilet thing in one corner and a sink. We'd been sleeping on the floor and cuddling close for warmth. We were all exhausted, frightened, dirty, and hungry, because the strange bars of tasteless stuff they'd given us to eat were barely enough to fill us up.

They were three other girls besides me: Jane Gardiner, Charlotte Lucas, and Lydia Philips.

We'd all been in the library at Longbourn College when the strange, bald aliens had come in the door, hit us with beams of bright light that knocked us out, and we'd woken up on a spaceship.

"What are they saying?" asked Lydia.

I shook my head. "It doesn't make sense to me." I thought maybe they were talking about the rainbow-colored aliens, the other species. They'd abducted us, and maybe they weren't supposed to do that.

If I could speak their language instead of only understanding it, I would have begged them to send us home, to end this strange nightmare.

"What do the Toth want with them?" said Ponytail.

"Repopulation," said Tall Blue. "Replace their women."

"Well, they're not unpleasant to look at," said Ponytail. He gestured at Jane. "This one is very pretty, if I don't say so myself."

"Indeed," said Tall Blue. "But this one?" He fixed his gaze on me. "I suppose I could tolerate it if a woman looked like her. Perhaps. I don't know."

I huffed.

He froze, narrowing his eyes, his gaze honing in on my ear. He made a noise in the back of his throat and looked up over my head, almost as if he were embarrassed.

Well, good.

"Let's take them," said Ponytail. "Let's take over the ship. We went past rooms and rooms of women like these. We could take over the ship and reroute it to Plembe and—"

"No," said Tall Blue. "No, we couldn't do that. As it's been pointed out, these humans being here is a violation of the Treatises."

"You can't take them back," said Ponytail.

Tall Blue knelt down and fixed his gaze on me. "Would you speak of this if we sent you home?"

My lips parted. "I'd answer you, but you can't understand me," I said in English.

His jaw twitched. "Ah, it's only a one-way translator, I see."

"What if we just take these?" said Ponytail. "The four of them?"

"We can't take people captive," said Big Blue. "What are we going to do with them?"

"We're just as in need of repopulation as—"

"We can't capture women and breed them against

their will. That's appalling. It's criminal. It's immoral. It's—"

"We'd be better than the Toth," said the third one, who'd been mostly silent until now.

Big Blue raised a six-fingered hand. "True."

"If we returned all of these women on this ship to Earth, their combined testimony would be enough to convince the entire planet of the existence of our galaxy, and it could have a detrimental effect on their development as a species. We can't—"

"Yes, I've read the Treatises." Big Blue sighed. "However, if we took control of the entire ship, it would be a declaration of war against the Toth."

"What? They're going to bomb us through the lectre field?" said Ponytail.

"No, but we'd never be able to leave again," said Big Blue. "We don't even know if these women are compatible with our species."

"But if the Toth are compatible with their species and we're compatible with the Toth—"

"Just these four," said Big Blue. He eyed me. "Will you come with us?"

I didn't know what to say.

"What are they saying?" said Lydia again.

I licked my lips and spoke rapidly, doing my best to explain all of it to them.

"They want to breed us?" said Charlotte, eyes the size of flying saucers. "I knew it was going to be a sex thing. Didn't I tell you that it was going to be a sex thing?"

"You did," said Jane. "You did, but they haven't touched us yet, and maybe—"

Big Blue was speaking again.

Everyone quieted.

"I'll promise that no one will harm you, and that nothing will be done to you without your express consent," he said. "You won't get an offer like that from the Toth. They're not particularly good to their own women. Well, they weren't, anyway, when they *had* women."

I relayed this to the other girls.

"So, they want to rescue us?" said Lydia.

"I like the long hair, to be honest," said Jane. "The bald guys are kind of ugly. If it's going to be a sex thing—"

Big Blue interrupted. "If you'll come with us, stand up and come closer to the door here."

I relayed this to the others.

"I say we do it," said Jane. "Anything's got to be better than this cage."

"I don't know," said Charlotte. "The blue ones are a bit bigger, aren't they? You think that means they'll be bigger… everywhere?"

Lydia just got up and sashayed over to the front of the room, beaming at the aliens through the bars.

Jane followed her.

"I guess I'm outvoted," said Charlotte. She stood up.

I did too.

Slowly, we moved forward.

Maybe we were a little nonplussed at this turn of events, but we'd been abducted by aliens less than a week ago, and everything was surreal at this point. We didn't have the energy to have emotional reactions anymore.

Ponytail gave Big Blue a look, and the third blue alien stepped forward and applied a long, thin metal sparking apparatus to the door. It shuddered, sparked some more, and then jerkily slid open.

We tumbled out.

"This way," said Big Blue. They ushered us down a corridor.

On either side, there were cells like ours, full of human girls in groups of three or four. They chattered as we went by, some in English, some in other Earth languages. Some reached for us. Some cowered. Some looked fine, others were bruised. Some of them were naked.

I reached back and took Jane's hand. She squeezed mine back.

None of us girls had known each other before we'd all been abducted. We all attended the same college and had been studying in the same library, late at night, when the place was about to close. I'd seen Charlotte on campus a few times. We lived in the same dorm. The other girls I didn't know at all.

Since living together and watching each other use the toilet for days on end, though, we'd all become close. I'd wager I'd never been this close to anyone, ever, since I'd never known my parents and I'd spent my childhood shuffled from foster home to foster home. I'd been officially adopted in my adolescence by a couple who made it their business to adopt older children, and they'd been very good to me, but it had been a crowded house full of their other adopted children, and when I'd turned eighteen, I'd had to go. They were emotionally supportive, and I went home for Christmas and Easter, but they didn't have the energy or time or resources to be like other parents might be, especially not when they'd adopted lots and lots of children over the years. I was grateful to them, but they had never felt like family to me, not truly.

Of course, maybe I didn't know what family was,

since I'd never really experienced it.

Even so, these last few days with these other girls, I felt as if there was a sisterhood between us.

Abruptly, Ponytail, who'd been leading the way, came to a stop. He held up a six-fingered hand, and we all stopped as well.

Big Blue came forward. He'd been behind us. "What is it?"

Ponytail pointed, and ahead, just around a bend, was one of the rainbow aliens—the Toth—with a gleaming silver gun-thing. He was a guard.

"I'll take care of it." Big Blue pushed past us, and we all watched him approach the guard.

They spoke—it was too far away for me to hear or understand—and they disappeared from view.

Ponytail waited a moment and then beckoned, and we all rushed down the corridor, streaming past the adjoining corridor where the guard and Big Blue had disappeared.

Then we came a set of doors.

Ponytail put his palm against a sensor-type thing on the side of the wall, and the door whooshed open, half of it going up and half going down. He and the other alien urged us through and we emerged in a vast, cold room full of spaceships. They were boxy and metal— much less sleek than the ones on *Star Trek*. More *Millenium Falcon* than *Enterprise*.

Big Blue appeared through the doors, and they closed with another whoosh behind him. "Let's go," he said, and took off at a sprint.

Ponytail and the other alien each grasped one of our hands, two human girls on each side of them, and they tugged us after him.

We clamored up over a ramp that slid down out of

one of ships and were shoved inside.

Big Blue found me and pointed at a set of chairs. "Strap in." He gestured. "Tell the others. We'll jump to deep space right away, and the straps will protect you."

Was that like lightspeed? Hyperspace?

I nodded at him to say that I understood. But I didn't know if nodding was a universal sign of affirmation. He did it back at me, nodding, but it was if he didn't know what that meant, so I guessed not.

"This is yes?" he said, nodding again.

I nodded, smiling.

He smiled too. So, maybe smiling was universal? I'd read somewhere that we smiled to show our teeth because it meant that we wouldn't actually hurt anyone, but I also knew that babies just started smiling at about three months, and maybe they were copying people or maybe it was just a natural way to indicate that they were happy.

Maybe Big Blue was copying me again.

I told the girls to strap in.

We did.

Charlotte sighed. "I knew it was going to be a sex thing."

"He promised us that nothing would happen against our will," I said.

"He could be lying," said Jane.

That was true.

"I don't know if I mind if it's a sex thing," said Lydia with a shrug.

"You wouldn't," said Jane, rolling her eyes.

Lydia had told us that her greatest ambition in life was to go to get an invite to the Playboy mansion, become Playmate of the year, and be universally adored. She'd even worked as a bunny at one of the

Playboy clubs, apparently.

Jane had said that Lydia was setting the women's movement back twenty years, and Lydia had said that using your boobs against men for profit was the most feminist thing ever, and Jane had said, "Not when Hugh Hefner makes more profit than you do off them."

I tended to agree with Jane, I had to admit. Anyway, I didn't think that sex was a thing people *should* sell, not in any way. It cheapened the idea of it.

Not that I could say that my own experiences with sex were all that vast or varied.

I'd had a boyfriend my freshman year of college and he'd had an off campus apartment, and it had... happened. I'd been a little disappointed. I'd read enough romance novels to think that it would be amazing, and I was as liberated as any other woman, so I wasn't a prude about it, but it had still been awkward, boring, and not all that pleasurable.

He'd assumed that since I let him have sex with him that we were going to get married, and I had not thought that far along, I had to admit. Not at all. When I agreed to have sex with him, I suppose I wasn't opposed to the idea.

And I guess the fact that the sex hadn't been very good shouldn't have meant that I soured on the idea entirely, but... well, maybe that was shallow, it just... The thing was, after we had sex, other things about him started getting on my nerves.

He had this way of exaggerating things.

When we first started dating, I suspected he was stretching the truth, because he would tell these stories about how he'd done all these amazing things, like he'd been the top of track and field in his high school and the valedictorian and the quarterback and he'd won the state spelling bee. I thought that he was probably making some of that up, and I didn't mind, because I figured he was just trying to impress me, and it was maybe a little flattering.

But then I started noticing how he would exaggerate when he was telling other people stories where I had been there.

And then, I was put in the awkward position of either agreeing with his lies or saying, "No, sweetheart, I don't think that's what happened, actually." Either way, I hated it.

And he also started listening to a lot of disco and wanting to go out to dance to disco.

I wasn't opposed to disco, necessarily. Sometimes, I could even get into it. But I was much more of an Eagles sort of girl.

Maybe I was just making excuses. The thing about marrying someone was that it was such a big deal, and it was so permanent. I really wanted it to be perfect when I got married. I wanted a family like I'd never had growing up. I wanted to be really in love. I wasn't willing to compromise in that regard.

Of course, what was I thinking?

I looked around the spaceship and remembered that I was being taken away by big blue aliens because they'd said that we could never go back to Earth, because our presence would break the Intergalactic Treaties or whatever. It sounded kind of like in *Star Trek,* when they weren't supposed to interfere with primitive cultures for fear of messing up their development.

Yeah, it was really uncanny how much *Star Trek* had gotten right.

Maybe Gene Roddenberry had been abducted and

brought back or something.

Huh.

On the other hand, maybe it really was all a hallucination. Maybe, right then, I was actually lying catatonic on a bed in a mental hospital, just dreaming all this up.

Did that mean I subconsciously wanted to be bred by a big, blue hairy alien?

I hunched up my shoulders.

Suddenly, the ship lurched forward and we all pressed back into our seats and then jerked forward into the straps, which held us tight.

"Hang on!" called a voice from the front of the ship. "We're making the jump to deep space."

TWO

darce

I opened cubbies in the belly of Blenge's ship, sliding the doors open, sorting through whatever was in there and then slamming them closed.

"Do you ever organize anything?" I said.

"Why are we down here and not with the girls?" Blenge lounged in the doorway.

I slid open another cubby, felt around inside, and *there*. I pulled out four two-way translators and held them up. "This is why."

"Oh, brint!" He yanked them all out of my hands and was out of the door and heading up towards the women before I could say anything else.

"Blenge, you can't just slap those in their ears, and we should probably be careful with them." He couldn't hear me. He was already out the door.

The humans were likely traumatized. They were a primitive species, with only a midlevel of technology, and they'd had no idea that there was other life in the galaxy. Knowing the Toth, they'd brutalized them. They could have already been raped or beaten or badly abused in some other way.

Ice gods knew, one or more of them could even be pregnant with Toth children by now.

I hoped not, however, because it seemed more likely

to me that the higher-ranking Toth would want women first, and they wouldn't take kindly to the lower class smugglers who owned that ship using the humans first. The hii graxes would want their new human women pristine and untouched.

I went after Blenge. He was younger than me. He was eager.

I understood. After all, unlike me, he'd been on Plembe all this time, while all of our women were either dying or barely recovering from the same illness that had plagued the Toth women. What women we had left were all sterile and fragile.

A planet of men without any women was…

Well, he was eager.

He needed to be careful, though, because he would scare them off. "Blenge!" I called.

"What?"

I caught up to him, and he was grinning at me, standing in the corridor outside the room where the girls were waiting.

"I saw the pretty one first," he said. "So, she's mine."

"Oh, brint. Let's not give any of them a choice," I said dryly. "Besides, we saw them all at the same time."

"Her skin's darker," said Blenge. "I like her the best. You're the blanic heir apparent to the high seat of the entire planet. You have enough going for you. Say it. She's mine."

"I promised that none of us would touch them—"

"I'll court her, of course," said Blenge. "I'll hunt for her. I'll bring her back the carcasses of—"

"Blenge, we don't even know what their own mating rituals are," I said. "Furthermore, we don't know what the Toth already did to them."

He went stock still, his expression twisting. "Oh, ice

gods of the horizon, I hadn't thought of that."

I snatched one of the two-way translators from him and entered the room.

I didn't know much about humans, so it was hard to know anything from their appearance. One of them, as Blenge had pointed out, was rather dark skinned, her skin a pleasing deep umber color. It was appealing, I had to admit. The other one, the one with the translator, was far paler, her skin quite light, with an odd smattering brown dots all over her nose. Her hair was brown, though it had a bit of a bronze look in the light, and she appeared, well, sickly, I thought.

The other two girls were also pale, but they had at least a bit of warmth to their skin tone. It wasn't as pinkish-white as the one with the translator.

Of course, there was something somewhat intriguing about the little brown dots. Did she have them everywhere? I wondered what she'd look like with all of her skin uncovered.

Such a thought was beneath me, however.

At any rate, Blenge was right that I was the heir apparent, and I did have a duty to my planet. A human girl was probably not for me, no matter what. I should marry one of the remaining furrne women, regardless of whether we could have offspring. It was the proper thing to do. It was what my aunt would want, undoubtedly. She ruled the planet now, and she would not be pleased if I shirked my duty.

I went directly to the one with the translator, and she was watching me warily too, probably because I'd been staring at her. I held up the translator. "This will allow you to speak as well. Can we replace the one you have?"

She fingered the translator in her ear and slowly

made the up and down motion with her head that indicated she agreed.

"Oh," I said. "You don't need to be strapped in anymore."

She relayed this to the other women, who all started to unstrap themselves.

Blenge knelt down on the floor next to the dark-skinned one, holding open his palm, which had the other three translators.

The girl with the dots was tugging at the translator in her ear, making a face.

"Ah," I said. "May I?" I reached for her.

She stiffened.

I stopped. "I'll just detach it," I said softly.

Her breath hitched. And then she made the up and down motion again.

I reached forward and my fingers brushed the shell of her ear. Their ears were more delicate than ours, with more intricate whorls. I found myself intrigued by the look of them.

At my touch, a shiver went through her.

Our gazes caught and locked.

Oh, well, she had eyes that were as green as the sky during mid pleicc, didn't she? They were... well... she was perhaps more pleasing to look at that I had first imagined.

I pinched the translator in her ear, and the strands inside retreated.

She let out a noise of surprise, perhaps a bit of pain.

I squeezed harder, and the translator came entirely free.

She touched her ear, wincing.

I handed her the two-way translator. "You put this in yourself, so you can adjust how far in it goes," I said, but then I realized she couldn't understand me now.

She seemed to get the gist, though, since she plucked it out of my hand and tucked it into her ear. She blinked, adjusting it a bit.

"Liz?" said the dark-skinned one.

The dotted girl turned to her. She spoke in her own language, gesturing for the other girls to take the translators, and then she turned to me, swallowed a bit, and then — in the language of my people — said, "Where are you taking us?"

"To the planet Plembe," I said. That probably meant nothing to her. She must have so many questions. First of all, though, it was only polite for us to introduce ourselves. I touched my chest. "I am Darce of the clan Firne, the heir to the high seat of Plembe. What are you called?"

"Elizabeth," she said. "Of the, um, clan Bennet. But we just say the last name."

"I can understand them!" said one of the other women, also in our language. She clapped her hand over her mouth. When she spoke again, I didn't understand her.

I turned to her. "It's a two-way translator, so it allows you to speak in our language as well."

"But how does it work?" said the dark-skinned one. "How does it know English?"

"It works by interpreting language in the brain, and it detects languages in a radius of seven claccs," said Blenge. "I'm Blenge of the clan Leye, by the way, and you're beautiful."

The dark-skinned one swung her gaze back to him. She let out a little laugh. "Um. Jane." She touched her chest. "Jane Gardiner. You're, um, quite handsome too. For a... a blue person."

Blenge burst into laughter, as if this were the most hilarious thing he'd ever heard in his life. "Oh, Jane, you're witty as well."

Witty? How was that witty? I ignored him and got the names of the other two women—Charlotte Lucas and Lydia Philips.

"What are you going to do with us?" said Charlotte.

"Nothing," I said.

"Where's the other one?" said Lydia.

"He's probably driving the ship," said Elizabeth.

"Yes," I said. "We'd say it, uh, flying."

"Oh." She blinked. "Flying the ship. Makes more sense."

"Well, there are only three of you," said Lydia. "One of us is going to get left out, and I say it should be Charlotte, because she's terrified of your big, blue cocks."

I stood up, letting out a noisy breath.

Blenge laughed again, a delighted laugh.

Elizabeth shoved Lydia and said something to her in their language. Lydia responded in the same language, defensive, gesturing with her hands.

I was mortified. I tried to collect myself, to say something, anything, to assure them that this was not some sort of—

"Lydia is blunt," Elizabeth interrupted my thoughts. "But I did overhear what you were saying, and there was a lot about, um, breeding."

I tried to collect myself enough to speak. "I promised that nothing would happen to you against your will."

"Right, but that *is* what you want us for?"

"No."

"Yes," said Blenge.

I glared at him. "*No.*"

"The species who captured you, they're called the Toth," said Blenge. "Their scientists were toying around with making weaponized viruses and one somehow was accidentally released from one of their labs. It infected their women and they all died. It was apparently targeted precisely only to infect women, not men."

"So, that's why they abducted us," said Jane.

"Yes," said Blenge.

"But what about your women?" said Elizabeth, looking at me. "You said something about needing repopulation as well."

"Toth women fled to remote parts of the galaxy to escape infection," I said. "We offered sanctuary on our planet, but some of the refugees were already infected, and the infection spread to our women as well."

"But how do you know that we would even be able to reproduce with you?" said Charlotte.

"We don't, necessarily," I said.

"But your species is compatible with the Toth," said Blenge.

"How do you know that?" said Jane.

"Our galaxy has been studying you for quite some time now," said Blenge. "The Toth especially has sent a number of scientists through the wormhole which leads to your galaxy. They will take a few specimens and put them through some tests and then wipe their memory and put them back where they found them."

"Specimens?" said Charlotte, her voice very high in pitch.

"Oh, perhaps I should have used a different word," said Blenge.

"You're very curious to us, you see," I said. "We don't understand how you could be so similar to us."

"Yes," said Elizabeth, sitting up straight. "That's very odd, isn't it?"

"Well, I don't think so," said Blenge. "It just means we're all created in the image of the ice gods, I suppose."

I groaned. "Blenge, truly, they don't even believe in our gods on Geheri." That was the Toth planet. "Let alone through the wormhole."

"Well, the ice gods must have traveled through the wormhole at some point."

"Or perhaps one of our species did," I muttered. "Then, over generations of time, they would have adapted to your planet, just as the species on the various planets in our galaxy have adapted to our environments, but we all have a common ancestor."

"You and your university ideas," said Blenge, with a snort.

"What makes more sense, Blenge, that we're all created by imaginary beings who live encased in ice or that the galaxy was settled by one species many, many mooncrosses ago?" I said.

"I don't think either of those things make sense," said Elizabeth. "Could it be possible that maybe, when life emerges, it simply takes a similar form? There are species on our planet, not as advanced as us, of course, but which are very similar to us. I can't think humans didn't originate on Earth."

I considered this. "Well, the origin of life is a mystery, granted. Blenge and I have agreed not to speak of it anymore."

"Because you're blasphemous," he said.

I shrugged.

Was Elizabeth smirking behind the hand that was over her lips?

I might like her. I might really like her a lot.

"But back to the matter at hand," said Elizabeth, "you do want us for breeding, then."

"I wouldn't put it that way," said Blenge. "It sounds sort of clinical, like something Darce would say."

I glared at him again. We were friends, but the fact that Blenge had never left Plembe and that he was a rustic in that way? It was sometimes annoying. Blenge said that I was arrogant and that I let my off-planet education give me airs. I said that he sometimes said very stupid things, and I wasn't going to be polite simply because he was too ignorant to know better.

Blenge was still talking. "We want you for courtship. We want to worship you and bring to you the pelts of a number of wilbeasts and iiciins, and earn your favor. We want you to choose to be with us. We want to make you our wives and partners. We—"

"Blenge," I said, shaking my head.

"Worshiping doesn't sound bad," said Lydia. "All of this about pelts and ice gods, though. Is Plembe a really cold place?"

"Well, yes," I said. "It's an ice planet."

"Oh," she said.

"You don't like ice?"

The women all exchanged glances and shrugged.

"We can't stand temperatures that are freezing," said Elizabeth.

"Neither can we," I said, pushing up my sleeve to bare the hair on my arm. It was scant. We had more hair than the Toth, but we were clearly brother species to them, because we were very similar. "We are not equipped for such temperatures either, but we have managed to survive on Plembe. The planet may be cold but it is warm inside our shelters and homes."

"And I guess there's no chance of us going to our own home," said Elizabeth.

"You mean your planet," I said.

"Yes," said Charlotte. "Can't we go home?"

"You want to leave?" said Blenge. "But you haven't even seen *our* home."

"We don't have access to the wormhole," I said. "It's controlled entirely by the Toth. To attempt it would be dangerous, and we'd probably all be killed."

"They'd recapture the women," said Blenge. "Then they'd do whatever it was they were planning on doing to you before. Speaking of which, are you all right? What have they done to you already?"

"They didn't touch us," said Jane.

"But those other girls we saw," said Elizabeth. "Some of them were bruised and naked and I… they weren't all as lucky as us."

"Lucky?" said Charlotte. "Nothing about this is lucky."

"True," said Elizabeth.

"Oh, you'll see," said Blenge. "You'll be very pleased when we arrive on Plembe."

I wasn't sure that they would be.

What we'd done, stealing these women from the Toth, it had been risky. Our planet Plembe was protected by a lectre field, and it was impossible for weapons or ships to penetrate it without help from inside the planet. On Plembe, a protective shield could be projected for ships with clearance, but it would never be granted to craft coming to do us harm, which the Toth might attempt to do if they became angry with us.

The nature of the field was one of the reasons that Toth women had come to take refuge with us, and another reason why the infection had run rampant through our women. Our isolation had worked against us in that regard. There had been nowhere to run to, not for us.

The Toth couldn't get to us, not if we didn't want them to. However, they could place us under siege, stopping anyone from leaving Plembe or arriving. They could cut us off from the rest of the galaxy.

Perhaps that wouldn't be such a terrible thing, what with the way the galaxy was changing. The Toth were grieved and maddened. They were violent and desperate, and they had been overstepping their bounds, breaking galactic treaties, seizing more and more power. The galaxy itself was crumbling.

Maybe the best thing for us would be to be cut off.

But not if we didn't have any women, of course, because we'd die off.

I doubted the Toth on the ship would much miss the four women we'd taken, but if they did, it definitely wouldn't have been worth it.

The first priority I had was keeping these human women safe. There were some men on Plembe who hadn't been in the same room with a woman in a mooncross. They'd be likely to do stupid things if they knew about the human girls.

We needed to sequester them somewhere secret, and we needed to do tests to determine whether or not we were even compatible for breeding. And then… well, if any of these women were willing to be with a furrne man of their choosing, maybe then we could move forward, maybe then we could…?

What?

There were *four* of them.

Four women for an entire planet?

And there wasn't much likelihood of the furrne people getting off our planet en masse to find wives amongst other species. This was due also to the nature of the lectre field, which meant that getting off planet was an expensive proposition. Going through the field required a good bit of fuel, and because of this, there were no public transport ships that landed on Plembe, and the only people who did leave were rich businessmen or rich members of the nobility.

Men like myself.

Blenge wasn't nobility, but he had a lot of credits from his business.

If I came back to my planet with four women and distributed them to the rich and powerful, the men who were the only ones who had a chance of finding wives, the lower classes would revolt. Those men wouldn't take it well, and we relied on them for all manner of services.

So.

What was I going to do?

It had been a very stupid thing to take these human women at all, I thought.

Very stupid indeed.

THREE

When we docked on the planet, Darce made us stay on the ship for a long time, and when he finally came back, he was alone. He told us we needed to be quick and quiet as he led us to something called a tirecraft, which would take us to where we'd be staying. It was a tall carriage-like vehicle with huge tires. Inside, it had comfortable, plush bench seats, facing each other and furs to wrap ourselves in.

Darce's desire for quickness and quietness was because he was trying to hide the fact that we were here from anyone who wasn't on a need-to-know basis, he said. He didn't elaborate, but the implication that I got was that all the men on his planet were crazed for women and if they knew we were here, he didn't trust them not to go insane and... rape us all to death or something?

I don't know.

It wasn't reassuring.

The thing about Darce?

He was inherently unlikeable.

Everything about him rubbed me the wrong way, and it wasn't because he said he could only barely tolerate looking at me. Really, it wasn't.

Okay, that hadn't helped.

He looked at me a lot, though, and it was a very uncomfortable feeling having his gaze on me, because he was clearly looking at me the way I might look at some kind of vaguely disgusting rodent or something. I could see that I fascinated and horrified him in equal measure.

Why he'd taken us from the Toth when he clearly was not the least bit interested in human women (and I knew this, because while he was implying we'd all be raped to death, he had said something to the effect of, "But of course you have nothing to fear from me, because I would never touch a human woman"), I couldn't say. I guessed we were meant to be gifts to other men on the planet, but really, why? There were *four* of us.

The way he'd spoken to Blenge hadn't endeared me to him either. He'd been very dismissive of Blenge's religious beliefs, which I thought was rude. I was agnostic about essentially everything. I didn't think that it was possible to know whether there was a creator or whether things had adapted and evolved. I had to admit that I thought evolution was more likely.

However, this other galaxy, with aliens that all looked like humans? It did more than anything ever had to make me wonder. Did similarities imply a common ancestor or did similarities imply a common designer?

I didn't suppose I'd ever know the answer to that question, but Darce's I'm-smarter-than-you attitude made me dislike him even more.

The tirecraft he led us to had wheels twice as tall as me, spiked to cling to the ice. We all climbed inside and strapped in and looked out the window as we were taken over the barren landscape. Out in space, it had been darkness as far as the eye could see. Here, it was ice and snow. There were some cliffs and craggy mountains off on the horizon.

The sky was greenish, and there was a sun that burned through it, meaning that the craggy mountains gleamed and glittered in the light in the distance.

It was actually stunningly beautiful, but I was in no mood to appreciate it, because Darce was getting on my last nerve. Well, to be honest, I was terrified. I'd been abducted from my home, taken to another galaxy, and then brought to a planet with aliens who wanted to breed me, and… and… well, it was kind of exploding my brain.

So, I wasn't focusing on it.

We arrived at a squat, rectangular building with long buttress-like supports on each side, which Darce said were there to protect against the winds, because ice storms could be very damaging. He pointed across the icy landscape at a much larger building, this one three stories high with rows of diamond-shaped windows, and told us that was Blenge's mansion, and that he would be staying there, and that if we needed anything, he'd show us how to contact him.

Then he took us inside and there was a female alien.

She was introduced as Fannee, and she waved both of her six-fingered hands over her head and shrieked, "Oh, ice gods of the horizon, ice gods of the *horizon!*"

Darce told us he'd brought Fannee here to look after us.

"My innards are all in a tangle!" she exclaimed. "I can't *breathe.*"

"She's excited that you're here," Darce said helpfully.

We'd noticed, but that wasn't what any of us wanted

to ask about, of course. But it seemed rude to say to Fannee, *How are you here? We thought all the women were dead.*

Lydia had no concerns about being polite, so she just came out with it. "I thought there were no women?"

"Oh, ice gods bless you, snookels," said Fannee. The two-way translator helpfully projected an image of a large, fuzzy cute animal in my head—apparently, a snookels. It was also a term of endearment. "It's true, three-fourths of the women perished. Those of us who survived are barren, can you imagine? That's why, seeing you all here, you're the hope for the future of the entire planet, and I…" She slapped a hand over her chest. "Oh, I'm overcome."

"She's overcome a lot," said Darce. "But she'll look after you, and she used to work in the capital helping women make matches with eligible men, so she'll be able to teach you all about our courtship traditions. If you wish to tell her about your own, please do. Perhaps accommodations can be made where possible."

"Oh, yes," said Fannee. "I'll have you all married and settled by the next mooncross, just you wait and see." The translator projected a picture of the night sky, two moons—one pinkish and one greenish—on opposite sides of the sky, across from each other. It must be some way to measure time, I supposed, like the way our months were originally based on moon phases.

Darcy left us to Fannee, who showed us all to our rooms. We each had a small room that contained a bed and we shared what they called a wasteroom at the end of the hall.

She also showed us an eating room that contained something called a duplicator, or that was how my mind translated it, anyway. It had a row of buttons like a keyboard over the top and a door below. She typed something in on the keyboard and the thing began to hum and cough. When it stopped, she opened the door and there were four bowls of something stewlike inside.

Apparently, the duplicator made food.

The stew itself wasn't bad, but it had a sort of odd taste to it that put me in mind of cafeteria food somehow.

After we ate, we gathered in Jane's room to talk, but all we really did was try to reassure ourselves that we'd made the right decision leaving that other ship, that we were going to be okay, and that we'd survive this. Charlotte spoke again of her family, her mother and siblings, but she didn't cry this time, even though every other time she had. She only said, in a resigned voice, "I can't believe I'll never see them again."

The beds were made of some kind of material that reacted to touch, molding around my fingers and making a perfect imprint of them. When I pulled my fingers away, it released, rippling out, almost liquid, to be smooth again. Lying down on it was the most comfortable thing I had ever felt. It hugged every dip and curve of my body, supporting me everywhere.

I should have fallen right to sleep, but I lay awake for a bit, trying to make myself understand I was never going back to Earth. I didn't have anyone to miss, not like Charlotte did, not really. But I'd had dreams. Plans. Hopes.

Some were stupid, like that maybe I could buy tickets to a Fleetwood Mac concert in September. But others were much more difficult to let go of. I'd wanted to go to graduate school and get my master's degree and become a librarian. I'd wanted to spend my life surrounded by books and to introduce other people to books.

All the books I loved were gone.

No *Emma*, no *Wuthering Heights*, no *The Sun Also Rises*, no *Farenheit 451*. Not even any *Carrie*.

This choked me up for some unfathomable reason, and I turned over in the bed, which adjusted to hug the front of me, and I cried into the soft liquidity of the comfortable bed, sobbed as if my heart had been ripped from my chest.

When I woke up, green light was streaming brightly through the window, and I got up and stretched. My body felt so much better. I'd been stiff and sore from sleeping on the floor on the spaceship. I looked out the window at the gleaming landscape, glittering against the green sky.

The other girls were in the eating room and there was another strange stewlike concoction to eat.

The big news was that Jane had been invited to Blenge's house for lunch.

By his sister.

"This is the way it's done," Fannee told us. "It's considered improper for a man to make an advance upon a woman if she hasn't given any indication that she is interested in him. But once she has formally acknowledged him, he can begin to court her."

"So, his sister is barren?" said Lydia.

"Sadly, yes, such a pity, for she's so young. And his other sister, poor Lise, died in an awful tirecraft accident along with her husband, and that couldn't have been too long ago."

"Oh, so he's experienced quite a bit of tragedy," Jane said, sighing.

"You're not going to let him court you?" I said.

"He's obviously very interested in her," said Charlotte. "He couldn't take his eyes off her."

"He said she was beautiful," said Lydia.

"Yes, but you don't even know him," I said.

"Isn't that the purpose of courtship?" Jane turned to Fannee. "It is where we're from, anyway. A man and a woman agree not to see anyone else, and they go on various outings together, often times to eat food in each other's company or watch entertainment. And then if they really like each other, they get married. How does it differ here?"

"Well," said Fannee, "women are allowed to court a number of men at once."

"Oh," said Jane.

"Yes, and I always encourage girls to try *everything* out, if you get my meaning." Fannee giggled wildly.

"You mean...?" Lydia leaned forward. "You're saying that's accepted here?"

"Oh, it's quite common for a woman to wait until she's decided to become pregnant to choose a husband, and I'd say quite a bit of the time, the husband she chooses isn't even the father of her first child," said Fannee.

I drew back. "And that's not a problem with the men?"

Fannee shrugged. "Well, some men are more sensitive to such things than others, but we do track inheritance through the female line, and usually by the time the second child comes along, the men are happy enough to know they've at least produced one offspring."

"So, you're saying that if I agree to court Blenge," said Jane, "that doesn't mean that I can't court other men, and that doesn't mean I can't have sex with other men?"

Fannee nodded. "Oh, yes, snookels. But the polite way to phrase such things is to say I can share furs with more than one man."

Share furs, I repeated inwardly. I should try to remember that.

We all looked at each other and burst into giggles.

"Don't the men get jealous?" said Charlotte.

"Oh, yes," said Fannee, smiling widely. "Maddeningly jealous. Sometimes there are fights. If it gets very serious, they may even challenge each other to a deathmatch, but it's no longer a deathmatch, because that would be quite uncivilized. It's a ceremonial thing mostly now. The men use specialized blunt knives called thoores, and they train with them from the time they are adolescents."

Jane cringed. "That sounds... well, I don't know if I would want men doing violence to each other over me."

"I would," said Lydia, brightening. "I love this planet so far."

I caught Charlotte's eye and we both snickered.

"What else do they do?" said Lydia. "Blenge said something about pelts."

"Oh, yes, men try to show their worth to potential mates by bringing gifts. This can be through hunting. That's very traditional, for a man to show how virile he is by bringing back a very large and dangerous beast. Or it can be other gifts, like clothes or jewelry or the like."

"I like that, too," said Lydia. "The clothes part, though. And the jewelry part. I guess furs could be okay. I was pretty opposed to the idea of killing animals *just* for their fur, but it's different if the whole animal is used, don't you think?" She looked at us for confirmation.

I could just picture Lydia as Cruella DeVil, trailing furs everywhere, smoking with a long cigarette holder, Anita *darling*.

But did I want some man to bring me fur?

I thought of Darce for some reason, but he seemed so fussy somehow. I could hardly picture him going out into the ice and killing things.

And oddly, I had to admit that the... how had Fannee put it? The virility of such an act, it did stir me in an odd way. I had to admit that a big, blue virile alien had a certain appeal, much more than disco-loving-compulsive-liar Biff.

The rest of the morning was spent getting Jane ready. Fannee brought out all kinds of different outfits for Jane to try on, most of which were long, fur-trimmed skirts, which seemed very pretty but not very useful for actually walking around outside in the ice.

Of course, I assumed that Jane would be picked up in the tirecraft and taken to the mansion. But Fannee said that wouldn't do, and she took Jane out back to a pen, where there were several furry animals that resembled a cross between oxen and horses, only covered everywhere in long fur, and she said that Jane must ride one there.

When Jane said she was afraid she'd fall off, Fannee only laughed.

A long discussion ensued. Fannee would not budge, and no matter what any of us said, it was apparently decided that Jane was riding a fur-ox to Blenge's house.

She was wrapped up in blankets and placed on a special saddle and we all watched from the window as she made her away across the ice.

She was nearly there when she *did* fall off.

We all let out a collective gasp of horror.

Except Fannee, who squealed in delight. "Yes, perfect!" she exclaimed. "Oh, thank the ice gods!"

We all turned on her, ready to express some kind of displeasure, but Charlotte said, "Oh, look, it's Blenge," and we all turned back to the window and there was Blenge, rushing out to scoop Jane off the ice, and *carry* her all the way to his house.

"Couldn't have gone better if I planned it," said Fannee.

"You did plan it," I said dryly.

News came back that Jane had actually sprained her ankle when she fell. Fannee had a communication bracelet and I asked if we could have them too. I thought they resembled the communicators from *Star Trek*, of course. Well, not in appearance, but in the general idea of them. There didn't seem to be any beaming, however, which was a pity. That would have been a more fun way to travel than by fur-ox. Jane was apparently going to have to stay overnight.

This sent Fannee into ecstasies.

But I was worried.

I felt close to all of the girls I'd be abducted with, but Jane and I were the closest. Some nights, when Lydia and Charlotte had been sleeping, we'd huddled in the corner of our cell and talked to each other for hours and hours. I knew that, unlike me, Jane had never had sex with anyone, and I knew she had expressed that she thought it was romantic to have only ever been with one man. I didn't want her over there with a hurt ankle, feeling pressured to do things she wasn't ready for with a big, blue alien.

So, I said I needed to go.

Fannee wouldn't hear of it, but there was a communicator in the hallway, and Darce had shown it to us, and I sent him a message on it that I thought Jane would feel more comfortable with another human there, and—within the next ten minutes—Darce appeared with a tirecraft to take me away.

"Oh, you didn't respond," I said.

"I assumed you'd want to get to your friend as soon as possible," he said. "Fannee! She needs a coat."

Fannee came over with a big, thick fur outergarment. Beneath, I was still wearing my bell bottoms and t-shirt I'd been abducted in. Fannee pointed at me with one long, blue finger. "Don't you interfere with Jane's courtship."

"Certainly, it's a bit soon for courtship," said Darce.

"Yes, exactly," I said. I actually hated agreeing with him about anything, but he was right. It was far too soon.

"I tried to tell this to Blenge, but he wouldn't listen." Darce sighed heavily. "Between the two of us, perhaps we can imbue a bit of sanity into them."

Them? Was Jane acting insane? I might have asked, but I didn't know if I wanted to hear him insult Jane. I didn't know if I'd be able to keep from hitting him if that happened.

So, I climbed into the tirecraft and off we went.

We were met at the door by Blenge and a younger alien woman, who had her long dark hair in braids that were wrapped around her head. She had her arms folded over her chest and her lips pursed. They were painted a deep, deep blue color that glittered. She had glitter around her eyes as well.

"You brought another one." She looked me over in

disdain. "What is she wearing?"

"Oh, really, Carle," said Darce. "These are the clothes they wear on their planet. I can only imagine how odd we look to them."

"Is this one diseased?" said Carle, who must have been Blenge's sister.

"Excuse me?" I said.

"No, I admit I did think that as well," said Darce. "I think the dark spots on her face are simply —"

"My freckles?" I burst out with. I looked back and forth between the two of them.

"Apologies," said Darce, clearing his throat, looking pained. "Carle is… understandably threatened —"

"I am not threatened!" Carle screamed this. She threw up her hands and stalked off, disappearing into the house, which was sleek and gleaming and had various things hanging on the walls that appeared to be sculptures or some kind of art. I just didn't know the plants or animals they resembled.

"It's brint to see you again, Elizabeth," said Blenge, coming forward and smiling. "Don't mind my sister." This was said with such a self-deprecating air that it immediately put me at ease.

I smiled at Blenge, who I was realizing I might actually like. He was much more friendly and warm than Darce, that was for certain.

"I suppose that having those, uh, freckles? Is that right?" said Darce.

I turned to him, giving him a glare that should have stopped him from continuing to speak at all. I had never liked my freckles growing up, but now that I was a grown woman at the ripe age of twenty, I had grown accustomed to them and to my entire appearance. Certainly, there were aspects of the way I looked that I wasn't fond of. I had frizzy hair that wasn't exactly red—it would be one thing to be a redhead, after all—and I had freckles everywhere and my breasts were smallish and my hips a little too wide to be entirely proportionate. However, I was lucky enough to have a small waist and I didn't struggle too much with weight. I could eat pretty much whatever I wanted. After being starved for a week on the Toth ship, I was actually svelt.

And anyway, I thought it was so boring and tired when women went on and on about how insecure they felt about their appearance. As far as I understood, confidence was sexy, and I tried to at least fake confidence when I couldn't actually muster any.

Darce was still talking. "Perhaps freckles are considered quite attractive amongst your people?"

I pressed my lips together.

"It's only that we have a childhood illness that produces similar sorts of spots and it's a bit alarming, that's all. We obviously will have a number of cultural and other differences between our species, and if we all take offense to every little slight—"

"I'm not offended," I said brightly. "How could a person *be* offended by being told she looked diseased, after all? No, that's definitely the *nicest* thing a man has *ever* said to me."

Darce's face jerked up and he looked over my head, chagrined, his jaw tense.

Well. Sarcasm seemed to translate, then.

I beamed, turning back to Blenge, feeling better than I had in days.

Telling off Darce made me feel oddly euphoric. "Can you take me to Jane?"

"I can and will," he said.

He looked as if he were trying desperately not to laugh at Darce.

Good.

FOUR

"Oh, you're not with the humans, thank the ice gods." Carle hurled herself down in a chair next to me.

I looked up from my bracelet. I'd been rereading one of my favorite novels, something written generations ago on Plembe. Many others wouldn't favor such archaic reading material, but something about it tended to soothe me. I enjoyed stories from history, not because history was a simpler time. Indeed, quite the opposite. Because history was just as complicated as things were now, only in different ways, and it affirmed to me that people were people and that we could triumph over difficulty if we were tenacious.

"How could you say that I was threatened?" She glared at me.

She wasn't going to let me read, was she?

"With her spots all over her face, and her sickly, pale skin, and those odd clothes she was wearing, and *everything* about her? I *couldn't* be threatened!"

Well, Carle, she does have a functional womb. I opted not to say this. I considered it needlessly cruel. I attempted not to be a cruel person, but I had to admit that no one would know if it they observed my interactions with Elizabeth Bennet.

Everything about that woman reduced me to idiocy

for some reason.

How could I have said that I thought she looked diseased?

I didn't think that. So, this was what I said, not that it was the right thing to say to Carle. "I don't think she looks diseased."

"Oh, of course you don't." She sniffed, throwing back her head. "Are you just like Blenge, then? Ready to capture her and take her off for a noonthe? Just think what your speckled offspring will look like."

I groaned. "I said she didn't look diseased, not that I was going to take her under my blanic furs."

She eyed me. "All right. All right, well, brint, then."

"She is… appealing, I suppose," I said.

"Is she."

"In a sort of exotic way." I was still curious about whether the freckles covered her entire body. I was curious about the entire topography of humans, I supposed. How did they compare to other species. What were their breasts like? They seemed similarly formed to our women, but did they —

"Exotic." Her voice was going guttural.

I turned to her. She looked ready to rip me to shreds. I winced. "It doesn't mean anything, what I think of her. It wouldn't be proper for me to court a human woman."

She relaxed immediately, smiling. "No, I supposed it wouldn't. You'll have to court a furrne. And with so few of us left, you'll naturally wish to find someone with whom you'll feel comfortable."

Yes, so we can die together and watch the royal line die with us. I sighed.

"You know, since you've been spending so much time with Blenge, you and I have become quite close, don't you agree, Darce?"

I looked up at her, horrified. What was *that* in her voice? Was that *always* in her voice? Perhaps I'd noticed it before, a time or two, but it had never been so wheedling and obvious before. She really *was* threatened, and I could hear the depths of her feelings within her tone.

I had thought perhaps she only had a passing admiration for me, but she…

I got up. "I need to…" I gestured. "Do a thing."

She got up. "A thing?"

"An important thing," I said. *Not sit here while you attempt to flirt with me, because I'm never, ever going to even consider marrying you. Never.* "To do with my position as the heir to the high seat of the entire planet. So, a very, very important thing."

"I see," she said.

"So, I'll go and, um, do it, then." I squared my shoulders and turned.

"Could I help?"

"No." I looked over my shoulder. "Definitely an alone thing."

"Oh," she said.

I winced. *An alone thing?* Ice gods of the horizon. I hurried out of the room.

I was never supposed to be the heir to the high seat of the planet. My cousin, Ane, should have ascended after the current ruler, my aunt Catte. But Ane had died from the sickness that affected women, and so had my mother, who was the next in line. My sister Gige should have been in line ahead of me, even though she was younger, as inheritance went to women first, but she had passed on as well, so the royal line was down to me and my cousin Rehke, who'd been with us on the ship when we stole the humans. He'd headed back to the capital while I'd stayed here with Blenge.

Anyway, if I'd had any thought this responsibility was going to fall to me, I would have done a better job of learning to, well, talk to people. I understood it was a thing that a ruler had to do. But now I was fully grown and I was forced to confront the fact I'd never really spent enough time cultivating much skill when it came to conversation.

I suppose I should marry a woman who could speak well. That would help.

I hurried down the corridors of Blenge's mansion, thinking these thoughts, and I was so preoccupied I nearly didn't see Elizabeth Bennet.

Then I did see her and only just managed not to plow right into her. I came to a stop, arms flailing. "Elizabeth."

"Darce," she said, looking me over. "Are you all right?"

"Perfectly fine," I said. My gaze skittered over her face, her freckles, her slightly upturned nose, and then down to the way her garments clung to her form, exposing the shape of her in a very pleasing manner. Embarrassed, I jerked my gaze up. "And you? Are you in good health?"

She laughed. "Oh, definitely. It's been, what? An hour since we've seen each other?"

Hour... It wasn't translating. Must be a measurement of time from Earth.

She was still talking. "My health has not changed in that time frame."

"Excellent," I said.

She simply stared at me, slowly shaking her head. "It is excellent, actually. You're right. It's good to be healthy."

"It most certainly is."

A pause.

"Well," she said. "This conversation has been *excellent* as well, but if there isn't anything else, I was—"

"Yes, where are you going?" I interrupted. "Are you leaving? You wouldn't attempt to walk out in the ice and snow, would you? Please, if you need to go, you must allow me to take you back in the tirecraft."

"Blenge has actually insisted I sleep here, and he said that he had some clothing that I could wear. I've been in this outfit for a week."

Week. Another Earth measurement. How long was that, I wondered? "What is a week?"

"Oh," she said. "Of course you wouldn't—" She furrowed her brow. "Well, on Earth, the moon appears to change shape because of the reflection of our sun, and that takes approximately thirty days, but seven doesn't really go into thirty, so I guess that's not why…" She paused. "Well, anyway, it's seven days. Seven Earth days."

I must have looked confused.

"Oh, days are a complete cycle of light and dark." She shook her head. "Well, day is the light part and night is the dark part."

"Ah," I said. "On Plembe, we refer to the light as pleicc and the dark as neicch."

"Pleicc and neicch," she repeated. "I wonder how long your pleiccs are to our days." She turned to look out a window. "It's starting to get dark now. I think they may be a bit shorter, but I couldn't be sure."

"It is darker for more hours than light now, due to the position of our sun."

"Oh, right," she said. "We'd call that winter, but I guess it's always winter here." She let out a laugh. "And never Christmas." She looked at her feet. "It's a holiday. Uh, a time when we don't work and we celebrate and have a big meal and give gifts."

"A feast time?" I said. "We have these as well. At the mooncrosses."

She smiled.

I smiled back, and I felt as if we'd shared something. For once, I didn't feel awkward and awful around her. But then I thought it must be sad for her, leaving behind everything she'd ever known. "You will miss your, uh, holeedaze?"

She smiled at the way I rendered the pronunciation, but she made that up and down motion with her head. "I will. Christmas is the most magical time, but on an ice planet, well, it might be like Christmas all the time." She let out a laugh. "I'll make the best of it. I always do. That's the way I am."

"I see," I said, and I did. I could see that she had a well of deep strength and determination within her, and that she was the sort of person who'd find some way to find the humor in everything. Hadn't she been a bit funny about the diseased comment, after all, with her sarcasm?

I might admire Elizabeth Bennet, actually.

I wasn't sure how I'd be reacting if I were in her situation.

She was holding up remarkably well.

I wanted to tell her this, but she was talking again.

"Well, I'm sure I'm the last person you want to talk to, so I'll be going to find my room and the clothes. Blenge told me it was just down this corridor." She gestured.

"The last person I want to talk to?" I repeated.

"It's all right," she said with a smile. "I don't really like you either." And with that, she walked past me, leaving me in her wake.

Oh.

Well, I don't know why that should hurt me so much, but it did.

She doesn't even know me, I said to myself. *I'm sure she'll get to know me better and come around to liking me just fine.*

Yes, so that she could meet some other man who would court her, maybe several men, and then she'd give birth to one of their children, and I would—

No, her not liking me was all for the best, on second thought.

* * *

elizabeth

I wasn't sure which was more upsetting to Carle of the clan Leye, that I'd been wearing human clothes or that her brother had given me some of her own castoffs to wear. She was shorter than me and larger in the bust area, so it wasn't a perfect fit, but my other clothes were probably ready to stand up and walk away on their own, so I wasn't about to complain.

I would have spent the entire evening with Jane, but she'd sent me off because she wanted to be alone with Blenge. She seemed to be developing some kind of crush on him, because whenever she talked about him, her voice got a little bit soft and admiring, and I wasn't sure what I thought about that.

She was adamant she wanted to be alone with him, however, so I left her.

I wandered around the house until I found Carle and Darce in a couch-laden room on the bottom floor. In the middle of the room, a cylinder was projecting up a holographic representation of a bunch of different sort of aliens—all kinds, ones I hadn't ever seen before—doing some kind of race in a glowing track that was suspended in midair.

Neither Carle nor Darce seemed to be paying attention to this, however. They were both scrutinizing different holographic projections that were coming out of their bracelets.

Darce seemed to be reading something.

Carle was not. She was looking at some pictures of gloves. She saw me come in and she got a horrified look on her face. "Those are my *clothes*," she said. Well, she practically wailed it.

Darce slapped down the projection of the words, as if he tucked it into the bracelet, and he gave me that look he always gave me, as if I were some strange, ugly thing he could not understand. "Elizabeth, so happy you could join us."

"Well, I'd be fine to entertain myself," I said. "If I were on Earth, I'd read or listen to music or something. Well, I'd probably have to be studying, actually. I was at school, and there were always examinations."

"Really?" He smiled. "I used to go to university."

I remembered something about that Blenge had said.

"After the tragedy here, with all the death, I had to come home, of course." He sighed. "I suppose your schooling was cut off, too, though, what with being captured by the Toth. It's a bit worse than having to come home and be a prince, so, my apologies." Except he didn't say prince. It was only that my translator turned it into that word for the first time.

And I might have stared at him, with my mouth hanging open, because all that heir business had not clicked for me before.

He was a *prince*, I realized. Of the *planet*.

"Elizabeth?" he said.

"I despise reading," spoke up Carle.

I closed my mouth. "Somehow, this doesn't surprise me."

She gave me a truly vicious look. "Yes, well, I'm sure you're too good to spend time conversing with the women on this planet. Too busy trying to get yourself in position under furs with all our men."

I nodded. "That's me, all right. I woke up one morning and thought that it would be absolutely wonderful to be taken away from everything I knew and brutalized and frightened, and all *just* because I wanted to share furs with *your* men. How did you ever guess?"

She let out a long, slow breath, her nostrils flaring.

Darce made a noise that might have been a cough or might have been a laugh.

I glanced at him.

His expression was entirely blank. "Well, I enjoy reading."

"Yes, yes, Darce," said Carle. "But you must admit that it's not an accomplishment that's worth much of anything for women, not these pleiccs. What good does it do us? Now, there is so much pressure on women on Plembe. We must be more than we have ever been."

Darce turned to her. "I suppose you're right. It is hard on the remaining women of the planet."

I suddenly felt guilty for being so sarcastic with Carle. I thought about what it must be like for her, to be one of only a few remaining women on the planet, but to be unable to have children. Facing down the extinction of one's species, it must be utterly horrifying.

I should give her a bit of leeway, I supposed. I couldn't imagine how I'd be feeling in the same situation, especially if a group of alien women showed up and all the men on the planet seemed keen on them.

To be fair, Darce seemed less than keen, so maybe that was a consolation for her.

"We rise to the challenge," she said. "Besides, I still say that we won't know for certain that I can't have children if no one ever tries to get them on me."

Darce sputtered. He got up from where he was sitting and moved behind the chair, putting a barrier between himself and Carle.

"What?" she said, standing up as well. "Are you all right? Is there something I can do for you?"

"I'm fine," he said very quickly.

"Maybe it's your bracelet. I'm clever with them. Let me see it. I can run a quick diagnostic and shut down any unnecessary processes that might be slowing it down."

"Thank you, but I always see to the maintenance of my own bracelet," he said.

"Yes," she said with a smile. "Of course you do. You're quite brint in that way, aren't you?"

He clutched the back of the chair with his six fingered hands, and I could see the tension all the way up his arms.

Well, this was interesting.

Carle continued, her tone downright simpering. "And I must say, I was watching you with that novel you were reading, and you read uncommonly fast, don't you?"

"I don't," he said, shaking his head.

I couldn't be sure, but I was fairly sure I was reading the situation here, and it was that Carle had an enormous crush on Darce, who wasn't the least bit interested in her and couldn't seem to figure out how to get her to stop. I found it hilarious, and since it seemed to cause them both discomfort, I couldn't help but enjoy it. I didn't like either of them. A little suffering on their part? Well, I wasn't going to complain.

Carle was talking again, her voice almost a purr. "As I said, I don't even like to read, let alone quickly like you."

"Well, it's lucky that I was the one who was reading and not you. I'm sure that this conversation about my, um, skills, is boring for Elizabeth."

Carle whipped her head around to glare at me. "Oh, yes, *Elizabeth*."

"I guess the translator isn't going to help me read your language is it?" I said. "If it could, I'd take a book and go. Really, I would."

"Well, there's a holoprojector in your room," said Carle. "You could watch vids if you liked."

"Like television," I murmured.

"How fast do *you* read, Elizabeth?" said Carle, a lilt in her voice.

"I don't… it hardly matters," I said. "I doubt I'm ever going to see a book written in English ever again."

"And as I said, it's not an accomplishment that is worth much of anything for women currently," she said. "No, obviously, what you human girls will need to do very well is simply spread your legs."

"Carle," said Darce.

She looked at him. "But not for you, right? You have to marry a furrne woman. It wouldn't be proper otherwise."

"True," he said, digging his fingers into the chair. "The turns this conversation has taken, however—"

"And what sort of woman should she be, the woman you marry?" said Carle.

His jaw clenched and released. "She'd need to be of royal blood." There was something pointed in his tone now.

She flinched as if he'd hurt her. "But certainly not necessarily, because how many women of royal blood even exist anymore?"

"She'd need to be educated in affairs of state and brint with diplomacy and well respected by the people of the planet," he said, glaring at her.

She drew herself up. "Of course. And added to that, skilled at dancing and entertaining, well-versed in the ways of etiquette and protocol, able to fill out the latest fashions and wear them well, and also able to converse politely on a number of subjects with a wide variety of people."

"And to all that, she must add something else," said Darce. "She must have education, perhaps an ability to speak other languages, and some familiarity with what is going on in the rest of the galaxy."

Carle sniffed.

Darce's voice lowered. "And I must, most importantly, respect her and be attracted to her. I must find her beautiful and charming and I must look forward to spending time in her company."

Carle flinched.

And I laughed. I couldn't help it. The two of them were in the middle of whatever ridiculous sparring session they'd cooked up between them, and it was funny to me.

They both turned to me.

"What?" said Carle.

I find your suffering amusing. "I don't think a woman

like that exists," I said. "Of any species."

She scoffed. "Are you so hard on womankind in general?"

"No," I said. "But any man who would be so demanding of his future wife would hardly be a man I could *tolerate*." I smirked, even though I was trying very hard not to.

Darce cringed, raising his gaze to the ceiling.

"You know, Elizabeth," said Carle, "even amongst my species, we have women like you. They are the kinds of women who say things like, 'Oh, I am so ugly!' in the hopes that some man will sweep in and contradict them and sing their praises."

I rolled my eyes. "That is not what I—"

"And I know for a fact that Darce hates that in a woman," she said. She turned to him. "I remember you saying that anything that smacks of cunning disgusts you."

Darce cleared his throat. "Well, when I said that, what I meant was—"

"Oh, yes, well, Darce is clearly disgusted by human women," I said. "That was never in question."

"Disgusted?" said Darce. "I don't know where you got that idea, Elizabeth, but I can assure you—"

"It doesn't matter, because you *must* marry furrne," said Carle, giving him a pointed look.

Darce sighed heavily. "I must. Yes. It's true."

"So, you see?" She gave me a look, triumphant.

"He's all yours, Carle," I said dryly. "I'm actually very tired. I think I'll go lie down." I didn't wait for either of them to say anything. I just walked out of the room and hurried out in the corridor.

I rushed away from them both, struggling to hold in my laughter. Only when I had rounded two bends did I stop, lean against a wall, double over, and let it all out.

I laughed until tears came to my eyes.

Oh, it served Darce right having that girl fawning all over him. It was exactly what he deserved. They were a perfect pair, the two of them. I hoped he did marry her. I hoped she followed him around complimenting how fast he read and offering to do maintenance for him while his jaw twitched and he dug his fingers into chairs.

It was delicious, really.

I hadn't laughed in…

Oh, not since being abducted, that was for sure. I should thank them both for being so awful and so dismissive of me, because at least it had become a good joke.

I *was* going to go lie down, though, but first I wanted to check on Jane. I had to wander around a little while until I got my bearings, and then I headed up a sort of elevator-type thing they called a transroom to get to the floor where Jane's room was.

Outside the door, I put my hand on the sensor there, because if you cupped your palm in front of it it would scan your hand and open on command.

Except I immediately heard noises from within that made me jerk my hand back.

I was stunned.

I backed away from the door and then rushed back to the transroom and back down to the lower level.

Where Darce was standing in the hallway. "Elizabeth, there you are. I've been looking for you. I want to apologize on behalf of Carle, and, well, myself also—"

"Did you know that your friend Blenge is currently *with* Jane?" It burst out of me.

"With her?"

"As in sleeping with her—sharing *furs*." I twisted my hands together. My heart was pounding.

He straightened up. "You're upset."

"I'm—" My heart thudded in my chest and my eyes stung. "Did you know?"

"I didn't," he said.

"You don't think that's awfully fast? We *just* got here."

"I do agree," he said quietly.

I let out several noisy breaths, trying to get my heart to stop beating so quickly. "I…" I shook myself. "You don't understand. Jane told me that she never wanted to ever be with a man like that until she was married."

"Oh," he said, drawing back. "That seems impractical. Surely that's something that should be tried out before making a commitment?"

My lips parted. "Well… well, yes, I agree, but Jane, *she* thinks—" I gestured. "On our planet, it's not acceptable for women to go around sleeping with a whole bunch of men before she gets married. Well… I suppose there's some disagreement about that, and we're trying to change things, but for a lot of people, a woman who does that she's…" I groped for words. "A loose woman, with questionable morals—" The translator wasn't translating any of those words. They were just coming out in English. "A whore." *That* translated.

His eyes widened.

I guessed that was an intergalactic concept. Wish I could say I was surprised. I licked my lips. "W-well, perhaps not necessarily that bad. But this is out of character for Jane, that's all I'm saying."

"Are you accusing Blenge of—"

"No?" I spread my hands. "I don't know."

"Well, he's not the sort of man who—"

"But what are his intentions towards her? And how could she just... just... she barely *knows* him. He's a different *species*."

"Truly, it's not..." He shifted on his feet. "Typically before such a thing would occur, a man would need to be accepted formally as a suitor by the woman, and that has obviously been skipped."

"Yes, Fannee told us that," I said, nodding. "So, this is... this isn't normal for you either."

"No," he said. "But it's an irregular situation all around."

"True," I said. A long pause, then I burst out with, "This is Jane's virginity. This is a very big deal. I just don't understand it."

"I'll speak to Blenge," he said.

I gazed at him. "All right. But what will you say?"

He considered. "I haven't quite figured that out yet." He grimaced. "But I brought you here, and you're under my protection, and this is my planet. I will fix this."

How would he fix it?

"Don't worry," he said, and he reached out, and I thought he was going to try to touch me to reassure me. But then, at the last minute, he hesitated, and I supposed he remembered that I was a disgusting human woman that he didn't like.

"I guess," I said, "that you'd never do something like that."

"Oh, no, indeed not," he said. "That's nothing like me."

"Because you don't even want human women."

"Well, I..." His facial expression froze, and his

mouth moved, as if he was trying to work out something to say, but no sound came out of his mouth.

"Because you think we're disgusting."

"I never said that word," he managed in a strangled voice.

"You didn't have to."

"Elizabeth, actually, when I look at you, I'm… that is… your freckles, they…"

I looked up at him, waiting.

He looked in pain, as if trying to speak was disrupting the internal workings of his body.

"It's all right," I said. "I'm not actually offended, and you don't have to try to say anything."

"But I want you to understand—" He broke off. "Actually, no, I decided it was probably better if you didn't like me, didn't I?" He rubbed his forehead, almost rueful. "Yes, you human women are disgusting."

Why did it sound like there was some tinge of sarcasm to that final comment? I blinked at him.

"I will speak to Blenge," he said, looking over my head as he often did. "We'll sort it all out. Try not to worry too much. Do you remember how to get back to your room?"

"Yes," I said.

"I can escort you if—"

"No, I'm fine. I wouldn't want to trouble you."

"It's really no trouble."

"Unnecessary, though. I'm quite capable of getting there myself."

"Excellent," he said, but that almost sounded sarcastic too. Shaking his head, he took off past me.

I watched him go, feeling admittedly confused. Darce was a very strange man.

FIVE

"Liz." Jane clutched my sleeve and pulled me down into a chair next to her. "I had no idea." Her ankle was bound with a shimmering bandage that seemed to have electronic readings on it. Every once in a while, it would beep. "You never told me it would be like that."

"Are we talking about alien sex?" I said. "Because how could I tell you anything? I've never done it."

"Oh, right," she said, nodding. "I guess I didn't think about that. Maybe it's really different with humans. What was it like when you did it with your boyfriend?"

I shrugged. "Okay, I guess."

"Okay? You guess?" She let out a long, loose laugh and scooted down in her chair, looking up at the ceiling with a blissful look on her face. "Definitely different, then."

"So, it was good."

She just groaned.

I crossed my legs, almost defensively. "Well, don't hold back there." I was actually curious, but I was also embarrassed and wary. I didn't know if I wanted to talk about this with Jane. It seemed so private.

She giggled. "I'm sorry, but really, Liz, it was... amazing."

I swallowed and lowered my voice. "Are they... how

do they compare to human men? I guess they have, uh, similar equipment?" It would have to be if we were compatible.

She nodded. "Yeah, but there were some extras." She grinned.

"Extras?" My eyebrows shot up.

"I think they're supposed to help him, uh, not slip out?" She lifted her hand to gesture. "He called them folioles. They kind of hook up over and then they brush against you, and it's..." Her eyes rolled up in her head and she shivered.

I could not picture this. "Hook? Ouch?"

"No, not like *in* your skin." She laughed, waving this away. "All around the, uh, the package?" She waggled her eyebrows. "They're just skin, and they get hard when the rest of everything else does, but they're also still sort of soft, and if you get one just in the right spot, it's brint."

"Brint? You're using their slang now?" I shook my head at her. "What is going *on* with you?"

"I thought you'd be happy for me." She gave me a funny look. "I like him, Liz. He's sweet and he dotes on me and he... I've never had a man treat me like that before. I can't even..." She groaned again.

"I'm not *not* happy for you," I said in a tiny voice. "But when we talked, you said you wanted to wait until you were married, and that you thought your virginity was a gift and that—"

"Well, yeah, I know, but that was before Blenge." She giggled.

"It was very fast," I said.

"Was it?"

"Yes."

"Look, Liz, we were abducted. By aliens. We can

never go home. Everything has been hell for days and days. Something good finally happened. I'm just trying to enjoy it."

"Okay," I said softly.

She leaned over and put her hand on my arm. "I'm sorry. You came to look after me, and I see your position. If we were at a party or something, and I said not to let me go home with anyone sketchy, you'd just be doing your friend duty."

"I'm only trying to look out for you. And the other people in this house, the ones who aren't Blenge, they're all… awful."

"Right? His sister?" She made a face. Then she took a deep breath. "But, on the other hand, can you imagine what she's been through? I'm sure she'll warm up to me eventually."

"Eventually, huh? I guess you've already decided to be longterm with Blenge?"

"Honestly, we didn't talk about that," said Jane. "We tried to talk. We really did. But then we started kissing and then… well…" She giggled. "It just happened."

"Don't you think you should talk?"

"Yes," she said.

"Well, that's all I want to say, then," I said. "Just talk. And if you're happy, then I'll be happy for you, I swear."

"I will talk to him," she said. "I will."

* * *

darce

"It just happened," Blenge said. He was gazing out the window, not looking at me, and he seemed preoccupied. "We tried to talk. We really did, but then we got… distracted." He let out a long, low chuckle and his face settled into a very silly smile.

I sighed. "Blenge. I have been talking to Elizabeth Bennet, and she's been explaining the culture to me. I think they, the humans, interpret sexual intercourse differently than we do."

"What do you mean?"

"I mean, you have basically just declared you want to marry her, I think. I don't know. She said that women don't have a lot of different partners, or that if they do, it affects their reputation?" I should have asked more questions, really. I would have, if she hadn't said that thing about my finding her disgusting, and I'd gotten tongue-tied.

He looked up at me, still grinning. "Well, I do want to marry her, so that's brint."

"It could be brint," I said. "But I have to ask... are you absolutely certain she was willing?"

His expression darkened.

"I'm not saying that you would ever do such a thing." Taking women against their will was the most taboo of acts, never tolerated. "But it's possible that you misinterpreted her, that's all."

"I didn't misinterpret her climaxes, all three of them," said Blenge.

I cringed. "All right, spare me that." I hesitated. "Although are they... similar to our women? Everything roughly in the same places?"

"Smooth almost everywhere," he breathed. "Except this adorable tuft of hair between her legs, covering her—"

"Never mind." I cleared my throat, shifting uncomfortably on my feet, finding—to my horror—I was getting aroused from that description, which was likely only because it had been mooncrosses since I'd had a woman. Who had time for such things when we were in the middle of a planetary crisis? "Erm, listen, Elizabeth said that this sort of behavior was unlike Jane, and she implied that perhaps you'd coerced her in some way—"

"Absolutely *not*." Blenge was incensed.

"Yes, but they may not behave like our women," I said. "Did she say it? Did she explicitly tell you she wanted you?"

He blinked several times, looking troubled. He turned back to the window. "I could tell that she wanted me," he said to the icy landscape.

"So, no," I said, sighing heavily. This was a disaster.

"She enjoyed herself immensely, I assure you of that."

"Yes, but that is not the point," I said. "Elizabeth said that Jane had never been with a man before. She said that virginity is significant in human culture, and your having... divested her of it, I don't know what that means."

"Oh," he said. "But she's a grown woman. How could she not have been through a number of courting seasons?"

"I don't know. It's different. They are not like us."

He slowly lifted a hand. "Well, I need to talk to her."

"I don't know about that."

"I have to clear this up!"

"If you coerced her, perhaps you frightened her."

"No."

"We are stronger and more physically imposing than our own women, Blenge. The human women are smaller still and so..." I let out a breath. "So oddly soft and fragile with their almost translucent skin—"

"Jane's skin is not—"

"What I mean is simply that it's not out of the realm

of possibility that you terrified her, forced yourself on her, and that she pretended to enjoy herself because she feared displeasing you."

His expression froze in a look of horror. "No." He shook his head. "No, I can't believe that. You weren't there. I *was*. If she had been pretending, I would have known."

"Would you?"

He hesitated. He turned to look out the window again. "I'm fairly certain I would."

"If she's afraid, the last thing we should do to her is put her in a situation where she's alone with you again. So, no talking, not yet, anyway. We need to slow this *down*, Blenge. They only just arrived. How could you...?" I clenched my hands into fists.

"It just happened," he whispered, sounding ashamed of himself.

"Well, don't let it just happen again," I said.

* * *

elizabeth

Jane and I waited for Blenge to come by again so that she could talk to him and figure out where it was that they stood.

But instead, Fannee arrived and said she'd be bringing us back in the tirecraft. She said she'd been summoned by Darce himself, who said we shouldn't be here anymore. Fannee clucked over this, saying it was a shame, and that she'd wanted Jane here—both of us here—for at least a one-ten, which apparently was short for one-ten-mooncross. Apparently there were three mooncrosses per cycle of the planet around its sun and dividing the time between mooncrosses into tenths was how they measured time. I assumed this was their equivalent of a week. It corresponded to nine pleiccs and neicchs. All this Fannee explained to us as we went across the icy field between the mansion and the building where we were staying.

I remembered that Darce had said he would fix things.

But, just like him, he'd only made things worse.

When we arrived back with the others, I sent him a message, asking him to get in touch with me again as soon as he could.

And then I didn't hear from him again for some time. We were kept busy being measured and fussed over and then we were brought clothes—shirts and pants that weren't unlike earth clothing. There were pajamas too, and underthings.

I told Jane to send Blenge a message, but she didn't. She said she wouldn't know what to say. I could see she was shaken by the fact we'd been dismissed from Blenge's house without a word, without even a goodbye from him. I tried to get her to talk about it, but she was quiet and turned inward, only saying things like, "I should have known better," and "Nothing good can happen to us anymore, can it?"

I determined that I was going to go back across to the mansion and talk to Blenge and Darce myself.

Except I couldn't drive the tirecraft myself because I didn't know how, and I was not getting one of those weird ox-ice-beast-things. (Jane's ankle was practically healed at this point. Whatever was in that shimmering bandage seemed to have accelerated healing in some way. It must be alien technology.) I wondered what would happen if I tried to walk. How cold was it out there? We'd been outside briefly and it hadn't seemed as if it were dangerously cold. I could walk it if I had good boots and enough warm clothes, couldn't I?

But then I got a message from Darce, which I listened to. He said, "You said this was all going too fast. I agree. I've convinced Blenge to leave to give you all space and time so that we can slow everything down."

Leave?

I tried to send him back a message, but when I did, all I got was a robot voice saying, "Bracelet is out of range of this short-distance communicator."

Perfect.

I could strangle that man.

I went to Jane and told her everything. "It's my fault," I said. "I overreacted, and he tried to fix it, but he's positively awful at fixing everything. Now, Blenge is gone."

"Gone where?" said Jane. "Is he coming back? Is he done with me?"

"I don't know, but it's because of Darce."

"No." She was grim. "The connection I thought we had? If we'd really connected the way I thought we did, Blenge would never have left me. No, I think I misjudged it all. I was stupid. You were right."

"I wasn't right about anything. I just jumped to conclusions, and I was upset, and I never should have done that."

"Don't blame yourself, Liz," she assured me, and I felt horrible that *she* was comforting *me* when she was the one with the broken heart.

The following day, we all noticed a tirecraft approaching on the horizon.

Fannee didn't know whose it was, so we all waited, hoping it was Blenge coming back for Jane. Well, that's what I was hoping anyway.

I didn't know, honestly. It had been fast. She had really jumped into things with him, very intimate things, before she even really knew him. But this was not the solution to that problem, not at all.

Maybe Blenge really was just insensitive, and maybe he should have insisted that he be allowed to talk to Jane.

Of course Darce was the prince, so maybe Blenge didn't have a say.

The tirecraft did not go to Blenge's mansion. Instead, it came directly to our door and two alien men in uniform got out.

One of them had his hair cut in a strange fringe across his forehead. He had a very grave expression on his face as he entered the building, one hand resting on a silvery-gun-thing that was in a holster at his side.

The other man's hair fell in ringlets around his face, and he was—quite honestly—the most handsome of the alien men I had seen thus far. His features were almost cherubic—though blue, of course—and when he smiled, it lit him up. He seemed to smile after everything the other one said, and I could see that he and I shared the ability to find amusement in other people's silliness.

"I am a member of the royal regiment," said the one with the fringe. "My name is Colle of the clan Bilne, and I was sent here personally by the holder of the high seat, Her Splendor herself, who allows me to refer to her as Catte, because she has taken quite an interest in me. Indeed, I believe this is why she entrusted this mission to me and allowed me to select my partner myself." At this, he turned. "May I present Wihke of the clan Iolne, another member of the regiment. He is not known by Catte, I assure you, but he convinced me that he was the man for the job, so I brought him along. Catte trusts my judgment, you see. She has the utmost faith in me, and for Her Splendor to give such an endorsement to a humble man such as myself is, you can imagine, quite the compliment."

"Her Splendor, the ruler of the planet, is aware of the girls?" said Fannee.

"Well, her nephew would have told her, wouldn't he?" said Colle.

Wihke looked away, as if trying very hard not to laugh.

"I suppose so," said Fannee. She turned to us. "That's Darce, of course."

Of course. I rolled my eyes. When I looked up Wihke was grinning at me, as if delighted by something.

"So, that is why she has sent us here," said Colle. "Well, me, and I brought Wihke along."

Wihke lifted two fingers next to his face, as if to say, *That's me.*

"Yes," said Fannee. "But why has she sent you?"

"To protect you, of course," said Colle. "Which we will do with our very lives. For there is no greater honor than the service of Catte, after all, and to die for Her Splendor would mean that I could die happy. I would wish for nothing more in my time on Plembe. Well, I suppose except to marry, which, as you all know, is no longer a guarantee, what with the women of our planet being so terribly afflicted and many gone from us. Tragically." He took a deep breath. "This, in fact, is something else that Catte has entrusted to me, the knowledge of the human women here, you all. I am to find out everything that I can about you, and perhaps she will reward me if I do so. She has indicated that I may be permitted to marry one of you."

We all drew back at this.

Colle beamed. "You, your skin. What is your name?"

He said this to Jane.

"Oh, this is highly irregular," said Fannee. "Why, women are allowed to choose their husbands, not the other way around."

"Certainly," said Colle. "I only meant, perhaps I could formally request to be a suitor to this lovely young human woman, so succulent and sweet."

Succulent? Was my translator misfiring?

Wihke snickered silently. He caught my gaze and waggled his shaggy dark eyebrows, which all the furrne men had. His were expressive somehow in a very appealing way, however.

I found myself grinning at him, almost helplessly.

"Now, now," said Fannee, "she's already had some interest. It seems ridiculous, really, that only one of these women is getting requests for suitors." She nudged me. "What about Elizabeth?"

I turned to look at her, horrified. "Me?"

Fannee patted my cheek. "I think those odd little spots of yours have really grown on me."

"Oh, for heaven's sake, they're called freckles!" I threw up my hands.

Wihke laughed out loud.

I turned back to him.

He grinned at me.

My breath caught in my throat. He really *was* handsome.

SIX

Wihke had the sleeves of his shirt rolled up, baring his hairy and thick forearms. His regiment uniform was tossed over a chair in the eating room. He had the duplicator pulled out from the wall and he'd taken off the back panel. He was working at it with various tools, concentrating and straining, and it was making the muscles in his arms move in mesmerizing ways.

"You're very skilled with that," Lydia said.

Lydia was here. It was just Lydia and me. Jane was in her room, and Charlotte was doing something with Fannee. Colle was outside, guarding the building.

"You think so?" said Wihke. "How would you know?"

"Well, you look like you know what you're doing," she breathed. "And you have to be very strong to do that. Your arms…." She looked at me. "Liz, don't you think his arms are kind of great?"

I blushed. "Um, Lydia, we shouldn't make Wihke feel embarrassed."

He looked up at us, arching one eyebrow. "I don't mind."

I blushed deeper.

His gaze found mine, and my lips parted and my mouth went dry.

"Just incredibly strong," said Lydia with a sigh.

He glanced at her, chuckling. "I think this is actually jammed. I'm not really trained with duplicators, if you want to know the truth."

"Well, we don't know anything about them," I said.

"No, we don't," said Lydia.

"And you seem much more well rounded than the other men we've met, like… like Darce, for instance."

Wihke snorted. "Darce would never dirty his hands with duplicator grease."

"No, he wouldn't," I said, lifting my chin.

Wihke eyed me. "You don't like him."

"Does anyone like him who's spoken to him?" I said.

He laughed, turning back to the duplicator. "I thought everyone loved him. He's the next in line for the high seat."

"He's arrogant, thinks he knows better than everyone else, rude, and awful in every way," I said.

"Tell us how you really feel, Liz," said Lydia, snickering at me.

I bowed my head. "Well, that's just my impression of him."

"It matches mine," said Wihke. "But usually he doesn't let people see that side of him. He has a public face. Underneath it all, he's kind of a jerk, though."

"Really?" said Lydia. "How do you know him?"

"Royal regiment." He gestured down at himself. "It's a family position. My father used to be his father's personal guard."

"Oh," I said. "I bet you've seen all kinds of things."

"His father, Sarre, he was a wonderful man. My father was killed tragically while defending Sarre, and Sarre stepped in and became like a father to me. He was… I loved him. He treated me like his own child. I actually grew up with Darce. We played together as children."

"Really," I said. "So, you know him very well, then."

"Very well," said Wihke. He jerked his head toward the tools. "Can you hand me…?" He pointed.

Lydia and I both scurried over to help.

He noticed this and laughed.

I stopped, gesturing for Lydia to do it.

He grinned at me and spoke to Lydia. "The one with two different attachments. It's red."

She held it up.

He took it from her, still grinning at me. "Thank you, Lydia." Wihke went back to the replicator. He wedged the tool under something back there and gritted his teeth, his muscles tensing in a delightful way… and then he dropped the tool, muttering a word that my translator let me know was a foul one. He wiped at his forehead and then reached back and — with one hand — pulled his shirt over his head in one graceful, gorgeous movement.

I fought the noise that wanted to come out down.

He was beautiful.

His chest was blue and gleaming, muscled all over and with a bit of dark hair clinging to him — just enough to accent his V-shaped body. His shoulders were glorious and enormous and defined.

My jaw had come unhinged.

"Well," said Lydia in a low, throaty voice. "You must have worked up a sweat."

"A little bit," he said, bending down to pick up the tool he'd tossed. "Where was I? Oh, yes, Darce."

"Darce," I repeated absently, trying to tell myself that it was rude to be ogling this half-naked man in front of me, no matter how perfectly he seemed to have been put together.

"He was jealous," he said. "He didn't want his father to care about anyone except him, and he never liked me. Even when we were children, he would do horrible things. Like, he'd break things and go and tattle and say I did it."

"Oh," I said, making a face. "How petty."

"Right?" Wihke shrugged. "But if it had stopped when we were children, it wouldn't have mattered. But it didn't. His father cared about me, like I said, and he even sent me off planet to university when I was old enough. He wanted me to make something more of myself than just being a guard. He told me he'd left me something his will, not a lot, but a little something, so that I could use it to start a business. But when Sarre died, I went to Darce, and he told me to forget about it, that I was never going to see a credit from him, and that I didn't deserve to take from his family more than I already had."

"Wasn't there anything you could do?" said Lydia. "On Earth, that would be illegal. An inheritance can't be taken away by someone else, not against the wishes of the person who made the will."

"Well..." Wihke grunted as he used the tool on the duplicator again. "I probably could have fought it, if I'd had any money to pay a lawyer, but I didn't. I had to drop out of school and find work immediately just to keep from starving."

"How awful!" Lydia turned to me. "Don't you think it's awful, Liz?"

I nodded slowly. I had to admit that—while I really didn't like Darce—this was even worse behavior from him than I would have predicted. "He let you starve?"

Wihke looked up at me. "He would have."

"Well, obviously, you didn't starve." I gestured to all of his uncovered, gleaming flesh. "You're very much alive." Plus, a person needed to eat to make muscle, and he'd clearly made lots and lots of muscle.

Wihke was giving me a knowing grin. A so-you-like-what-you-see grin.

I blushed again, hunching up my shoulders. "Well, I don't like him. I've never liked him."

"You have good instincts, Liz," said Wihke, and his voice had gotten pleasantly deep.

I met his gaze. "I do like to think so." Why had my voice gotten all breathy like that?

Lydia let out an annoyed breath.

I turned to look at her.

Wihke went back to the replicator. "And, you, Lydia, seem to have all sorts of brint qualities too."

"I do?" said Lydia, perking up.

There was a popping noise and a large sheet of metal came off the back of the duplicator. Green sludge spilled out of it, oozing onto the floor.

I let out a surprised noise and so did Lydia.

"That's the problem," said Wihke, setting down the sheet of metal and the tool. "This is gunked up in here. Looks nasty, but it should be an easy fix."

"Really?" said Lydia. "Wow, you're really handy, aren't you?"

He laughed softly, under his breath, and when he looked up at me, I got the impression he was laughing at Lydia, that he and I were sharing a little joke.

* * *

darce

"I'm only saying that I'd like to send her a message or something," Blenge was saying. He was pacing in the sitting room of his town house in the capital city of

Roise. We'd all left and come here, which had seemed like the best idea at the time. "I know what you were saying before, Darce, about her being frightened, but with the distance, certainly, she and I could get through it all and sort it out?"

"No," said Carle, who was sprawled out on a couch, sullen, scrolling idly through pictures of dresses on her bracelet. "I don't know what you're thinking. You can't marry a human."

"I think that's up to her," said Blenge. "It's always up to the woman. No one's asked her what she wants at all."

"I think Carle's right," I muttered.

Blenge turned on me, looking furious. "What do you mean? Why did we rescue them, if not to—"

"All right, listen, there are four of them," I said. "A man like you, marrying a human woman, would cause a stir. Just imagine it. You bring her to a gathering or a dinner party, and just think how wild all of the men of the nobility would go over the prospect. What are we going to do about that? There is not enough of them to go around."

"Well..." He thought this through, rolling his shoulders. "Well, all right, then. I won't parade her around."

"So, you'll marry a woman and then keep her locked up, hidden from everyone, your dirty secret, your plaything?"

"No!" He was furious. "It wouldn't be like that. It wouldn't be against her will. It wouldn't all be about... sharing furs. It would be a marriage. I like her. I like talking to her."

"Right, because you did so much of that." I was sarcastic.

"You're not being fair."

"And you're thinking about yourself and not about the good of the entire planet, and I *have* to," I said. "It's my job. Besides, when I spoke to Her Splendor about the women, she had a suggestion I had not thought of."

"What?" he said.

"Artificial insemination," I said. "It doesn't seem to make sense to limit the genetic material of the offspring of these women to one male with each of them. This way, they could have offspring with a number of men. It would be more diverse, and it would be better for the population—"

"That's much worse," he said in horror. "Forcing them to be pregnant constantly through clinical means? I suppose they'd take their children from them and give them to furrne women who can't have children. That's disgusting, Darce."

I lifted a hand. "Perhaps."

"Perhaps?" said Blenge. "It's—"

"All right, I made promises to those women that I would not allow anything to happen to them that they didn't choose, and they will be given a choice," I said. "But when I present to them the idea of living in constant fear of some desperate furrne man trying to capture them or living in relative safety, I can't say *what* they might choose."

"Jane would never choose to give up her children," said Blenge. "Of that I'm sure. I need to talk to her. You've cut me off from her—"

"This was your own decision," I said.

"I think it's disgusting, Blenge," said Carle. "You've lost your mind."

"Maybe I have," he said. "Maybe she's driven me mad. Maybe I've fallen in love with her."

"You barely know her," I muttered.

"Even so, what I felt for her, what we shared, I think it was powerful. And I need to talk to her."

I sighed. "I'll make contact, and I'll find out how she feels about you, whether she wants to talk to you or not. All right?"

"You promise me?"

"Would I lie to you, Blenge?"

He eyed me for a very long time and didn't answer.

"I wouldn't," I said firmly.

"You have your priorities," he said finally. "I know you put the well-being of the planet ahead of your friendships is all."

I bowed my head at that. I wished I could say it wasn't true.

Unfortunately… I did have my duties.

* * *

elizabeth

There was an entry query at the door to my bedroom, and I hurried over to push the button to accept it.

The door slid open and there was Wihke. He wasn't wearing his uniform jacket. He seemed to never be wearing that. His shirt beneath was half open, baring a hint of the dark hair on his chest and rolled up to show off his thick forearms. "You busy?"

"Aren't you?" I tried not to stare at his bare flesh. "Don't you have duties you should be seeing to, like… guarding things or something?"

He arched an eyebrow. "I've managed to make some time. Can I come in?"

"Sure." I stepped back.

He sauntered over the threshold, into my bedroom, and the doors snapped shut behind him, enclosing us here together, alone. He wandered through the room, taking in its blank walls and the lack of furniture. There was really only a bed in here. He sat down on it, scooting backwards and leaning into the wall. He looked very comfortable. He grinned at me.

I clasped my hands together in front of me and stayed near the door. "Um… what can I…? Did you need something?"

His grin widened. "I don't know if need is the right word."

Oh.

"But was that an offer?" He raised his eyebrow again.

My heart started to beat faster. I blushed. "I… uh…" I felt dizzy.

"Come sit next to me."

My heart was still fluttering away, like a trapped thing with wings. Should I say no? Was there a reason to say no? If there was, I couldn't think of it.

"Unless you don't want to." Now, he was sitting up straighter. "Ever since I got here, I've been feeling like there was something between us?" He laughed a little, sounding embarrassed. "Maybe that's ridiculous. It's nothing I can point out other than a handful of looks and a few shared laughs. Maybe it's wishful thinking."

"No." Oh, my face was so hot. I took a step toward the bed. "No, I feel it too."

He leaned back into the wall, smiling again, looking pleased, like a satisfied cat. "Brint."

I took a deep breath, summoning my courage, and then I crossed the room and perched on the edge of the bed, next to him.

He gazed at me openly, greedily. His voice went deep again. "I can't believe Darce didn't stake his claim on you right away."

"Me?" I squeaked it.

"Your clearly the prettiest one."

I let out a laugh—and it was an awful, embarrassing, braying one. "No, no, everyone likes Jane. Jane is the prettiest. Everyone thinks I look diseased with my freckles and my pale skin."

"No," he said. "You're incredibly exotic." He was a little breathless as he leaned forward again. His hand darted out and he barely touched my hair. "The way the light comes through your hair, it illuminates—"

"My frizz."

"It's like you're glowing."

I blushed again.

"Do your kind kiss?"

My breath caught in my throat.

"Almost *everything* kisses," he said. "What sentient species doesn't pursue pleasure, after all, and what species doesn't have a sensitive tongue?"

I still couldn't breathe.

"So?"

I nodded wordlessly.

"And can I kiss you?"

I lifted a shoulder, trying to breathe, trying to speak, trying... I nodded again. And then I remembered that furrne didn't nod, and he wouldn't know that I was—

His mouth on mine.

I let out a noise—an embarrassing guttural noise—into his mouth.

He swallowed it, his thick, strong arms going around me, pulling me against his firm, warm chest, crushing me against him. His tongue licked against the seam of my lips.

I parted them and let him into my mouth.

His tongue was agile and thin and intriguing. It was large and it tangled with mine—truly tangled, seemingly wrapping around my tongue, everywhere at once, licking the bottom of my tongue and the top, which made shudders go through me, and the tip went against the roof of my mouth, a sensation that wasn't the least bit bad.

He pulled away, but his hand had somehow gotten into my hair, and I hadn't noticed. He twined strands of my hair around his fingers. "Like a Toth," he murmured. "But all the Toth women are dead now. You even taste like a Toth."

I wasn't sure what to say to that.

He grinned at me again. "Sorry, it's just... I've never... you're so different. I'm trying to find some way to even make sense of you."

"Me too," I whispered. Something surged in me, some odd bit of bravery—it wasn't really like me—and my hand darted out and I put my fingers on his chest, on the skin that was bared where his shirt was parted.

He liked that, letting out a pleased noise. He settled back against the wall and pulled me with him. He touched either side of his shirt, where it parted. "It's an eazclasp. You can simply pull it apart." He gave me a teasing look. "If you want to, of course."

I swallowed, blushing.

He touched my face.

I pulled open his shirt. I ran my fingers all the way down his chest, over every solid swell of him, every ripple of his abdomen. He was beautiful, and I liked the way he felt under my fingertips. I let out a little gasp.

His hand left my face and cupped my breast.

I gasped again, surprised.

"Can I?" Could he what? Touch me? He was. It

didn't feel bad or anything, but this was all... it was very fast. Had it been like this for Jane?

He pushed up my shirt and pulled aside the bra-like garment I'd been given. Fannee called it a supporter. Just like that, one of my breasts was bare. He squeezed it, letting out a noise, his hips coming up in a thrust.

That was when I realized he had an erection.

His, um... it was there, under his pants, and it was straining and big and very stiff and...

He chuckled. "You want to see?"

I looked up at his face.

"I don't mind," he breathed, and he opened his pants, and there it was.

It was blue. The tip of it was deeper blue, almost black at the very end. He had a foreskin like a human man—a blue foreskin—but it was pulled back because he was so, well, hard and swollen. There were little veins pulsing against it, and it... it was very similar to a human's, actually, just the color was different and maybe it was sort of enormous, but I thought I could take it. Easily.

That thought rippled through me and made my body react in surprising and pleasant ways.

Then I noticed the folioles that Jane had been talking about. They seemed to come up out of the base of him, and they were about as big around as my pinky finger and nearly as long. They curved, and I thought they might curve around my labia if he were, well, inside me.

I could see that one of them might curve right up and slide just against my clitoris, and my eyes widened. I touched it, rubbing my thumb over the tip of it and then under the curve.

He let out a little breath.

"Does that feel good?" I whispered.

He took my hand and wrapped it around his shaft, tightening my fingers around him. He kissed me again, fierce and hard, and his hand moved over my hands, urging me to stroke him.

I complied. We were doing this, I guessed.

His kisses were hot and wet and overwhelming, and I panted and rubbed him and massaged his interesting, agile tongue with my thicker and blunter one, and he groaned into my mouth, deepening the kiss, cupping the back of my head, holding onto me—

There was a beep on his bracelet.

He detached, letting out an unintelligible sound of annoyance. He touched my hand, stopping me from where I was stroking him.

I let go of him.

He pulled up a string of alien characters on his bracelet and then typed something back, making a face.

Another set of characters came back immediately.

"Ice gods of the horizon," he muttered. He kissed me again, quickly. "I've got to go." He bent down and planted a kiss on my breast, the one he'd bared.

I gasped.

"We'll, uh, we'll continue this," he said, his voice a dark promise. "Later."

I nodded. "Yeah," I said breathlessly.

He caressed my breast, sending a tingle of sweetness through me. He kissed my lips again. Then he rubbed his forehead against my neck, very slowly and deliberately. He pulled away and looked at me. "There."

"There?"

"Scented you." He touched my nose.

"Oh," I said. "What does that…?"

He shrugged. "Nothing. It's nothing. If you had other suitors, they might get annoyed, but you don't."

"Are you my...?" I furrowed my brow. "I thought there's supposed to be some kind of asking, and that I was supposed to accept?"

He kissed me again. "Will you accept me as a suitor?"

I blushed again. "I mean, obviously." I laughed helplessly.

"I really have to go." He tucked himself away—he was still hard—and he put his clothes back in order.

One last kiss, and he was gone.

I flopped back on my bed and gazed up at the ceiling.

What had just happened?

SEVEN

darce

When I arrived at the building where the humans were being kept, I was not pleased to be greeted by a man who told me his name was Colle. I'd never heard of him before, but he seemed to have somehow wormed his way into the graces of my aunt, and rather deeply too, for no one was allowed to call her Catte. And yet, this man did call her that. He went on and on for some time about my aunt and things she'd said.

On one point only did I think to question him.

"She said you could marry one of them?"

"Well, she did not say that in so many words, but she spoke of it as a possibility, yes," he said.

"But she was quite clear to me that she didn't want any of them married, and that putting human women out into the population would be calamity for everyone."

"Well, if it were only one," said Colle, smiling widely. "If the others were not known of. I'm sure a story could be concocted of a wreck on the planet, only one survivor."

"What?" I said. "I am going to speak to my aunt about this."

"Oh, please do." He smiled at me.

If there were only one survivor, how did my aunt

think to explain where the babies were coming from, I wondered. Perhaps she'd leave the humans out of it entirely and claim that she'd found some way to grow babies in a lab, using human DNA spliced with furrne. It was the kind of thing the Toth might be able to do, after all.

But they couldn't.

If they could, they wouldn't need to abduct human women.

On the other hand, I wondered if that were so. Maybe the Toth derived some pleasure from capturing and forcing women. The Toth culture was male-centric, heavily violent, and focused on conquest. Until now, they'd mostly kept it between themselves, but lately, they'd turned their ire outward.

I left Colle, troubled, and I went looking for Elizabeth.

I found her in the eating room, standing in the front of the duplicator, staring at it in a very odd way.

I stood in the doorway. "Elizabeth?"

She startled and turned to me.

"Apologies. I didn't mean to frighten you."

"Darce!" This was forceful. She wasn't happy to see me.

"Something wrong with the duplicator?"

"No, it..." She looked back at it and her whole face and neck got reddish, making her freckles turn darker. "I was just thinking about..." She shook herself. "Never *mind.*"

That was puzzling, but it hardly mattered. I took a deep breath. I tried to collect my thoughts about what to speak to her about.

She seemed a little flustered, twisting her hands together, now looking everywhere except at the duplicator. "You just up and left."

"You indicated to me it was all happening too fast. I remedied that."

She scoffed. "You can't possibly think that disappearing is what I thought you should do. Poor Jane."

"This was all done in service of Jane," I said. "You said—"

"I know what I said," she interrupted. "That's not the point. You don't need to repeat it to me." She tilted her head to one side and looked me over. "What sort of person are you?" It was as if she were saying this to herself, not to me.

"I'm the sort of person who's trying to protect the women I foolishly stole from the Toth," I muttered.

"Foolishly?

"It's created nothing but trouble, quite honestly."

"Oh, so sorry to be a bother!" She glared at me.

"I didn't mean it that way, I only…" This was not at all going well. It was impossible to talk to this woman. "Let's speak of Jane, then."

"What is there to say?"

"Did she go willingly under the furs with Blenge or did he coerce her? That is the crux of the matter, I think."

"Right." She squared her shoulders. "Well, she said it was fast, and that she wanted to talk to him about the future and whether he meant for it to mean anything, but I don't think she was unwilling."

"The future," I repeated.

"Yes, does he want to marry her? Or was he just using her for novelty? He didn't ask to be her suitor."

I let out a breath. Here was the crux of it, then. I could tell the truth, that Blenge was eager for Jane, or I could conceal it. One choice meant betraying my friend and these women I'd just met. The other meant betraying the well-being of the planet. What was I going to do?

"You know, I haven't talked to her about this, but I've thought it, and what if she's pregnant already?"

"Ice gods of the horizon," I said, stunned. "You're like the Toth."

"Why does everyone keep saying that?"

"You can get pregnant year blanic round," I said.

"Do your species go into season or something?"

"Yes."

"Oh." She blinked, as if trying to make sense of this.

"Women's bodies are equipped to store sperm that they, er, collect, and the strongest, most positive attributes are the ones that are favored when the body begins its fertilization."

"Really?" She shook her head. "How are our species still compatible, then?"

"We don't actually know that we are," I said. "I need to have tests set up. How often do your kind cycle?"

"Uh, every twenty-eight of our days," she said. "Which I think are somewhat similar to the pleiccs here."

I lifted a hand. "Well, when I get the compatibility tests set up, we can obviously determine whether or not she's with child as well."

She made that motion of affirmation by moving her head up and down.

"I suppose that's what I need to see to." I glanced over my shoulder. "I guess I'll—"

"*Can* Jane speak to Blenge?"

No. Not yet. I needed to sort through all this. I couldn't agree to allowing her to become his wife.

Taking those women off that ship had been a terrible idea. Why had I done it? Why had I been so impulsive? I was never impulsive.

Was it Elizabeth?

That was an odd thought. Certainly, she was very intriguing and alluring in her way, and she did seem to turn me into a stammering idiot, but…

Well, when I first saw her, I didn't think anything of her. I couldn't have taken those women just because I wanted her under my furs.

Ice gods of the *horizon*.

I was never sharing furs with this woman. Why would I even think such a thing?

"Well?" she snapped.

"Hmm?" I said.

"You're just standing there, silent, saying nothing."

I scratched the back of my neck. "Yes, yes. Apologies. I suppose I'm distracted."

"By what?"

Embarrassed, I looked up at the ceiling, avoiding her gaze.

"Oh, I don't even know what to think about you. Things that I have heard about you, coupled with my own observations, I can't seem to make sense of it."

"Heard of me?" I looked at her again. How could she have heard things about me? "From Fannee? She and I barely know each other. And I just met Colle, so I hardly think he'd have tales to carry."

"There's another guard here from the royal regiment," she said. "You know him very well, I understand."

"Who?" I said.

"Wihke of the clan Iolne."

I went entirely still. He *couldn't* have come here.

"The way you treated him, after you grew up together as children. The sufferings he's endured—"

"Oh, his sufferings have been great indeed," I said, sarcastic, unable to stop myself. I turned around, ready to go and find him, because of *course* he'd come here. It was exactly the sort of thing he'd do, and I should wring his neck or at least bloody his nose or possibly—

"So, is there some other side to this story?" she said. "And what about Blenge? You still haven't said if Jane can speak to him."

I backed away, into the hall, looking one way and then the other, as if Wihke was just going to appear in front of me and I would—

That *smell.*

I turned back to see that Elizabeth was close, coming for me. "Wait. You will finish speaking to me, Darce."

My whole body went slack in a kind of painful feeling of utter disbelief. No.

"What?" she said, angry.

I took her by the shoulders and pulled her close. I buried my nose against her neck and breathed it in. I felt like sobbing. "He blanic scented you." I let go of her. "You let him—no, you don't know what that means. You have no idea." I wanted to scent her over it, just try to wipe it out. I wouldn't, of course. She wasn't mine, and I had no claim—

"What does it mean?" She was wide-eyed.

"It's only for a wife," I whispered. "Doing it against a woman's wishes is practically a crime. Doing it when a woman has other suitors is a declaration of war."

"War?" she repeated.

"Well, a fight, anyway." I looked her over. "Has he…? You were…?" I swallowed. My voice came out as a rasp. "He *touched* you."

"What do you care?" she said.

I only shook my head.

"Darce, you're acting very strangely at this moment," she said. "The thing with Wihke, it was sort of fast, I guess—"

I let out a wild laugh. "Very fast." I let go of her and stalked out into the hallway.

"Where are you going?"

"You don't know him," I said in a tight voice. "You don't know anything about him."

"Well, why don't you just *tell* me, then?"

I opened doors, looking inside, bellowing Wihke's name.

"What are you doing?" said Elizabeth, behind me, following me.

The other women all came out, also wide-eyed, looking frightened. I didn't care. It was most important to get him away from them as quickly as possible.

I burst through the door at the end of the corridor, and he was outside.

I yanked him in, slamming him up against the wall.

He laughed at me from inside his furred hood. "Why, it's Darce."

"I won't have you in the royal regiment," I said.

"Oh, yes, take every job opportunity from me," he said. He leaned around me. "You see, Liz? You see how he is?"

I looked over my shoulder at her.

She was right there, looking distressed.

"You will stay away from the human girls," I said softly. I let go of him. I squared my shoulders. "And you will not scent—"

"Oh," said Wihke in a different voice, his smile taking on another quality. "Well, then. So, it *is* like that."

I glanced at Elizabeth, who seemed horrified and angry and confused.

"Did you know that those freckles of hers fade out over her breasts like—"

"Stop," said Elizabeth, turning to Wihke.

Wihke ignored her. "Think of that, then, Darce. Get a nice picture of me with her. You can add that one to the picture you have of me and Gige, eh?"

Bile rose in my throat.

"What *is* this?" said Elizabeth.

Wihke turned to her, putting one long finger in her face. "He takes everything from me, and a man can only take it for so long before he feels the need to take something back from a bully like that."

"I assure you, Elizabeth," I said, "that is *not* the way—"

"But you and me, Liz, you felt it too," he said to her. "So, you know that's real, and it's nothing to do with him. I'm sorry I taunted him. I shouldn't have. It's only that you have to understand—"

"Stop talking to her," I said. I took him by the arm and tugged on him. "That's quite enough."

Elizabeth wrapped her arms around her waist, stunned and crestfallen.

I dragged Wihke away from her.

"What am I supposed to do against the heir?" Wihke yelled, letting me drag him, not fighting me at all, which was his way, anyway. He was a coward when it came down to it. He'd never attempt to fight me. "He has all the power. He's the one who's taking me away."

I threw him out of the front door and back towards the tirecraft I'd come here in.

"Where are you taking me, Darce?" he said.

"Elsewhere," I said shortly. I really should kill him. I wouldn't, not on account of the fact that my father had loved him, that I had… that a long time ago, he'd been like a brother to me. But I *should* kill him.

* * *

What had just happened?

Jane had her arm around me, and the other girls were close too, asking me questions, but I was just… sobbing. I didn't even know why. I didn't mean to cry. It seemed like the stupidest thing to cry over. Why didn't I cry when we got abducted? Why didn't I cry when the Toth had shoved me into the cell or when they'd put the painful translator in my ear? Why over *this?*

Jane stroked the back of my head, holding me against her. "Don't crowd her, all right? I don't know what happened. I don't know anything. She can't answer anything while she's crying."

"I'm not crying," I said through my tears.

Jane laughed a little. She patted my head. "Okay, you're not crying. Come into my room, though, Liz, and we'll talk about it?"

I let her bring me in there, and we sat on her bed, and my tears stopped, and I started to explain it all. I went through everything I could, and then I stopped and took a deep breath.

She looked at me, her brow furrowed into a look of concern. "It wasn't like that with me and Blenge."

"What?" I said.

"You said you were wondering if it was like that, like the way it was with you and Wihke, and it wasn't."

"Oh," I said. I paused, thinking that through. "Well, how was it different?"

"He just… made you touch him?"

"I didn't mind." I shrugged. "I guess that was sort of… he didn't really ask if I wanted to."

"Blenge just touched *me*," said Jane in a low, affected voice. "Touched me all over and he did things with his tongue—"

"Okay, well, maybe you don't have to tell me everything," I said.

"You were pretty graphic," said Jane.

"Was I?" I cringed. "Sorry."

"Anyway," she said. "That thing Wihke said to Darce, about your freckles—"

"I know." I grimaced, feeling that rip through me again. It had been horrible to have him just burst out with some description of my body like that, about my breasts. That was gross of him, and I had *not* liked it. "But he did apologize for it. And I guess he just wanted to make Darce angry, although it's stupid, because Darce is not into human women, and me least of all."

"So, you think it's true, that Darce is a bully who takes things from Wihke?"

"You think it's a lie?"

"I don't know." She spread her hands. "I guess I want to think the best of everyone."

"You're not thinking the best of Wihke. He didn't do anything I didn't like. And the sex stuff was kind of hot, like how much he wanted me."

"Right." She nodded. "I can see that." She paused. "Is there some way they can both be right? Maybe it's a big misunderstanding."

"I don't know," I said. "I don't know."

"I never even thought about being pregnant." She studied the inside of one of her palms. "All I've been doing is wondering if Blenge cared about me or if he used me. How could I not have thought of it?" Now, she sounded like the one who might cry.

"Hey." I put a hand on her shoulder. "It was only once. I doubt you're pregnant."

"I hope not." Her lower lip started to tremble. "It would be terrifying enough to be pregnant and alone without it happening on an alien planet."

"Oh, Jane." I was the one hugging her now.

She buried her face in the crook of my shoulder. "How can this be our *life* now, Liz?"

Tears came to my eyes too.

"We're *never* going home," she said, and her broken sobs echoed off the walls.

EIGHT

The next day, there was a replacement guard, a man named Forste, who was married. His wife had come along with him, and they both took up residence together in a room they shared. His wife and Lydia seemed to hit it off nearly immediately, and they spent a lot of time together, giggling wildly over things that the alien woman would show Lydia on her bracelet.

They brought with them some kind of handheld scanners which Fannee dragged over our bodies as they projected blue lights and emitted lots of beeps and whistles.

Jane was not pregnant.

We were definitely compatible with the furrne.

Humans were apparently highly compatible with a number of known species. The list was very long.

"Lucky you're here and not being fought over in the depths of the galaxy, snookels," said Fannee, tittering.

Jane didn't seem pleased that there was no baby. She cried, saying that she knew it was better this way, but she felt as if she had nothing now.

No word came from Darce.

Definitely nothing from Blenge.

And Wihke was gone too.

Jane hid in her room for several pleiccs and Lydia

spent all her time with her new friend, and so it was only me and Charlotte.

"I'm older than the rest of you, you know," Charlotte said. We were sitting together in a room that had a holoprojector, but we weren't watching anything. The shows and vids that we could put on seemed too fast and too slick and too much. They were nothing like what you could watch back on Earth. "I'm twenty-seven."

"That's not old," I said.

"I'm not saying it is," she said. "But, you know, maybe this is all for the best. Back on Earth, I'm obviously nothing special. I'm approaching old maid status."

"At twenty-seven?" I said.

"How old was your mother when she had you?" said Charlotte.

"I don't know," I said. "I never knew my mom. I grew up in foster care."

"Oh, gosh!" She gave me a pitying look. "I'm so sorry." Then she considered. "Maybe it's lucky, though? That you didn't have anyone to leave behind?"

"Yeah, I've thought that too," I admitted. "Awful as it sounds."

"It's the time now to think all sorts of awful thoughts," she said. "My mother had her first child when she was eighteen. And she was not considered young at the time. My dad was shipping out for World War II, and she didn't even know if he'd come back. He did, but not before she had my sister. I was the fifth kid in my family." She sighed. "I don't like to think about how I'm never going to see them again, but I like to remind myself that this means no more Christmases with everyone asking me when I'm going to settle down, and no more looking at my sister and her kids and feeling that ache inside me, like, when do *I* get a kid?"

"Do you want kids?"

"So much."

"Really?

"You don't get it. You're twenty," she said, sighing. "When I was twenty, I was too busy working and doing my own thing to think about kids. And then, I don't know, just a few years ago, I suddenly woke up and decided to go back to college, and then one day, around the same time, they were just everywhere."

"What was everywhere?"

"Babies."

"What?"

"I mean, they obviously were there before, but I didn't notice so much. Suddenly, all I could see was babies. Suddenly, it seemed like everyone had one except me. All of my friends from high school? Married. Lots of them having their *second* kid, or even third. And there I was, all alone, with nothing to show for my entire life except having spent my early twenties waitressing and now being in college with a bunch of girls *your* age."

"I'll have you know, I'm very mature."

Charlotte laughed. "You actually are."

"This thing with Wihke, it may not make it seem like I am, but..."

"I don't even know what exactly happened with you and Wihke. Jane is the only person you talked to, and she sure hasn't explained it to the rest of us."

"Well..." I thought about it, trying to sum it up. "He asked to be my suitor. I said yes. We did some, um, things?"

Charlotte snickered. "Things, hmm? Talk to me about the alien *things*, if you know what I mean. Or did the things you did not involve inspecting that area of his anatomy?"

Heat rushed to my face and I looked away, also snickering.

"Did you... what do they say, share furs with him?"

"No," I said. "I think we maybe would have, but he got interrupted."

"Oh, yeah, I remember that Colle was annoyed because he wasn't at his post."

I furrowed my brow. He said he'd made time to see me, but he'd been avoiding his work during that time?

"Liz? Did I make you uncomfortable?"

I turned back to her, shaking the thought away. "I did see it. I, um, touched it." I grinned at her, a smile too big for my face.

She smiled a smile back equally as wide. "And?"

"And there are... extras."

"What?" She lowered her voice. "What do you mean?

I tried to explain the folioles, gesturing to my own pelvis, showing her with my finger how one of them sprouted just out of the middle of his groin, and how I thought it would very perfectly brush against a woman's clitoris.

Her eyes got very wide. "Ohhh..."

Then we were both quiet.

Charlotte finally took a deep breath. "Well. We've been captured by aliens and we can never go home. Our lives are not our own. We're being sequestered and guarded, for our safety, supposedly, but we're still prisoners. So, basically everything that's happened to us in the past several weeks has been a nightmare. The extra-alien-anatomy, though? That's *fantastic.*"

I burst out laughing.

She did too.

We laughed and doubled over and clutched each other.

When our laughter finally died out and we lay gasping, half falling out of the seats we were sitting in, she looked up at the ceiling and said, "Maybe it's fate."

"What is?"

She sighed. "I wanted babies, Liz. I wanted them so bad. And here we are, and we're surrounded by pretty blue men who just want to put babies in us. So... maybe this somehow the answer to everything for me."

"But if we have babies with them, they're going to be... well, different than us."

"That's not going to matter."

"No," I said immediately. "It really won't."

"You're young and pretty," she said. "They're all sniffing around you, and they're sniffing around Jane. If I get a chance at one of them, I'm taking it."

"But Charlotte, there's a *planet* full of them. You could probably afford to be choosy."

She considered. "Maybe." She sat up in her chair and looked down at me. "What about you? Are you waiting around for Wihke to find his way back to you?"

I slid further down in my chair, putting my hands over my face. "I don't even know."

"You like him, right?"

I nodded, still covering my face.

"But that Darce guy doesn't seem to like him."

"Yeah, and he's the prince of the entire planet."

She drew back. "I did not know that."

I uncovered my face. "Neither did I, but yeah. He's going to, like, run the place, I guess. I don't really understand their government. We should ask Fannee."

"She probably doesn't even know," said Charlotte. "Doesn't seem like the type to pay attention."

"Well, for that matter, I couldn't teach a government class in the U.S. I know the basics, but not the ins and outs."

"Good point," she said. "So, you don't think Wihke *is* coming back?"

I didn't say anything.

"Or you're just trying not to think about it at all."

"Well, I don't know anything, and I can't do anything. I'm helpless!" I clenched my hands into fists. "And Darce, he makes all the decisions. For me, for Jane, for everyone, and he doesn't have the *right*."

"Yeah, we can't stay here forever," she said. "We're effectively prisoners, no matter what they say. And they tell us that we're better off than when we were with the Toth, but are we? We have no way of knowing that."

"Well, the Toth were going to force us—"

"They hadn't forced us. No one had done anything to us."

"But those other women we saw, the bruised ones—"

"True." She sighed. "It doesn't matter. It's not as if we can do anything about it. We can't go home. We can't even leave this planet. And it's so icy and cold out there, we can't even really attempt an escape on foot."

I nodded.

She let out a long, low laugh. "It's funny, really."

"What is?" Because nothing about this seemed actually funny to me.

"Well, if you'd explained this situation to me, I would have imagined myself like some kind of hero from the movies, right, fighting my way out and stealing a spaceship to go back home?"

"We can't do that."

"I know," she said. "It's funny how quickly you adapt to things. How easily you accept changes to your environment. How soon it is that you're ready to work within the new framework to get what you want."

"But what do you want?" I said.

"Freedom," she said. "Babies. A life. Out of this place." She looked around. "If I were you, I'd forget about Wihke. I think you're right. He's never coming back."

* * *

darce

I was delayed getting back to Blenge and Carle by having to deal with Wihke.

I did what I always did with him, it seemed. I gave him money.

I stuffed his account full of credits and told him to go away. He begged to be allowed off the planet, saying that he couldn't be forced to be stuck here on a dying rock where there were no women.

"There *are* women."

"And they're all spoken for and guarded fiercely."

"I should have you put in prison."

"Always with the threats," he said.

"And no matter what I do for you, you're never grateful," I said.

He scoffed.

"Stay away from the human women," I said.

"You should really learn to flirt, Darce. She might not have been so ripe for the taking if you'd gotten in there first."

"Flirting, right." I just glared at him. "Is that what

102

you did, or did you just shove her hand into your pants and scent her against her will?"

"Think what you like. She and I have something. You'll never understand it, because women don't like you as a general rule."

And then I just let him go.

I didn't even hit him, let alone seriously consider killing him. Ice gods, from a certain point of view, one might say I rewarded him, because of all those blanic credits I gave him.

The problem was that Wihke still felt like family to me, even though he'd proved to me that he was nothing of the kind. And of the people I'd grown up with, he was all I had left. Parents gone. Sister gone.

I had every reason to hate him, and I did hate him. But I loved him, too. That was the problem. He was still my brother in so many ways, and I couldn't…

As for Elizabeth Bennet, I had no reason to feel the way I did about her. She was utterly unaware of my admiration for her, although perhaps that wouldn't be true anymore, not after the way Wihke had taunted me in front of her. She must have realized…

Oh, how embarrassing.

Maybe that was when I decided what I was going to say to Blenge. I don't know. Maybe I'd decided it a long time ago, even before I went to inquire about the truth from Elizabeth. Maybe none of that had mattered.

Blenge was right.

I did have my priorities, and the planet meant something.

But I had to admit that the way I treated Wihke was irrational, sentimental, and possibly harmful to the entire populous. He was not a good man. He should be in prison or dead or… well, he was never going to change. I knew it. Why did I keep giving him chances?

It was only that when it was your brother—

Except he was *not* my brother.

"She's terrified of you," I said to Blenge.

He and I were alone, in a game room where he'd been batting away holographic spaceships with holographic laser beams. He yanked the apparatuses off his arms that projected the lasers. "What? She said that?"

"She didn't want to see me either," I said. "I spoke to Elizabeth."

"But that can't be. Darce, you weren't there, and I was, and I can assure you, there was nothing—"

"It's better this way, Blenge. We can't have four human women mixing with our society, not when our entire planet is really dying. Think of fifteen mooncrosses from now, or even further into the future, fifty mooncrosses? Think of where we'll be when the children we have now are grown, when those boys come of age to no one." Younger girls had not been immune to the disease, unfortunately. It had been a tragedy on a wide, wide score. "Think of what's going to happen here."

"Well, it's not just happening here, Darce. It's happening to the Toth as well, and there were other species affected to various degrees, perhaps not as badly as here, but we'll find a solution. We're not dying."

I shook my head at him. How could he delude himself in that way? It was as if the truth was so awful he couldn't face it.

Maybe most people were that way, when it came down to it. They lied to themselves.

"If it were that dire, things wouldn't be going on as

they are," said Blenge. "Why, we'll go off planet. We'll find other women of other species."

"That's perhaps a solution for the rich, Blenge, but you know most of the population can't afford it."

"So, you'll give them the fuel."

"Give them…? How can I do that? I don't own the fuel."

"I'm sure those who do will donate it."

"Would you donate your product for no compensation?"

"Certainly," he said. He considered. "Well, a portion of it, anyway. I can't give everything away. It would bankrupt me, and then I'd be useless, and I couldn't pay my employees or buy more raw materials or…" His face fell. "Ah."

"Giving away fuel cripples the economy and collapses society faster," I said.

"Well, what are we going to do then?"

"I spoke to you about the artificial—"

"But that's borderline criminal, Darce." He shook his head. "Besides, if there aren't enough of them to go around, there aren't enough of them to populate the planet."

"Well, it's better than what we have now," I said.

"Are you certain I can't speak to her?"

I couldn't meet his gaze. "I'm very sorry, Blenge. But it's best if you forget about her."

"And I'm not even allowed to *speak* to her?"

"She doesn't want to speak to you," I lied, even though Elizabeth had asked several times for that precise thing, even though it was exactly what Jane wanted.

His face twisted.

I looked away.

For the good of the planet, I told myself. But maybe I was choosing to be strong and stalwart and to behave rationally in this way only because I needed to balance my utter idiocy when it came to Wihke.

Sorry, Blenge.

I left him there and Carle was loitering near the door to their house in the capital. She teased me about when I'd be offering as a suitor for "the spotted one."

I was terse but polite and didn't respond to the teasing.

I left, and I knew I wouldn't be welcome in Blenge's home for some time, that he would associate me with his heartbreak. I deserved it, and I would bear my punishment.

For the good of the planet.

* * *

elizabeth

"It is my intention," said Colle in his overly-grave voice, "to stick very closely to you, Elizabeth Bennet, for the rest of my break time this pleicc, I think, and indeed, every break time for the foreseeable future."

Oh, no.

I shook my head at Colle. "But whatever for?" He and I were in the eating room. The duplicator was fixed now, but not because of Wihke. He'd broken it and left it like that. It was Forste, the one whose wife was Lydia's new best friend, who'd fixed the duplicator. Now, it was capable of making coffee, spaghetti rings, and oatmeal, which were things that the Toth had apparently programmed it to do in order to make it easier for human women. Based on their observations, they'd thought these would be the things that Earth women wanted to eat, I supposed.

Spaghetti rings.

They were indistinguishable from the Chef Boyardee Spaghettios. They even had the oddly metallic-tasting meatballs.

I'd maybe been eating them for breakfast, lunch, and dinner every day since the duplicator had started making them, but even still…

"Don't play coy," he said, laughing at me, interrupting my thoughts. "In fact, I must say, Her Splendor, Catte, she has much to say about coyness in women, and she does not hold with it at all. Best to be candid and clear and to lay everything out."

"All right, then," I said. "I'm not interested in you."

He squared his shoulders. "Well, Her Splendor and I have conversed on this subject as well, many times, and I know that it is a common practice for women to play a little game and pretend to be uninterested. All the better to whet the appetite of the man for the chase. I know you've already been pursued by Wihke, and this does make me want you all the more, of course." He made a noise in the back of his throat that I thought was supposed to be sexy.

It was not.

"I assure you," I said. "This is not me playing hard to get."

"You'd say that in any case," he said. "You, Liza, are stunning."

Liza? Who'd told him to shorten my name in that way? No one, that was who. I glowered at him.

"Also, perhaps, I should explain my reasons for wishing to court a human woman," he said.

"No, I think that's pretty obvious," I said.

"I think it will greatly increase my happiness to be married," he said.

"Of course you do."

"And furthermore, I think it's good for all men to have a woman in their lives. And as you know, there are not enough women to go round on our planet, not anymore. Now, Catte has taken an exceeding interest in me, as you may know."

"And why is that? Because you're actually annoying. Is the queen of the entire planet idiotic, or perhaps just annoying and oblivious also?"

"How dare you? Her Splendor is, well, full of splendor. And she has given me special dispensation to choose amongst you the companion for my future life. Furthermore, I think the blending of our interspecies romance will be an example to all. And Catte has indicated how proud she will be of me in this enterprise."

"It seems to me you should marry Catte, then."

He snickered. "A preposterous idea. She is already married."

"Oh. So, how does her husband feel about her exceeding interest in you?"

He drew back. "Why, Liza, you cannot be suggesting there is something untoward between me and Her Splendor, can you?"

I seethed. "I'm really done with this conversation."

"Besides, tragically, Her Splendor's husband died many mooncrosses ago."

"So, then she *could* get married?"

"No."

"Why not?"

He ignored this question. "Her Splendor advises me that a human woman will not be like the other women on the planet, who have a high opinion of themselves since they are in such scarcity. No, a human woman will simply be grateful that any man of my species pays any attention to her. She will not be so high and mighty and she will suit me quite well in this regard."

"Yeah, I don't see why you would think that. If the entire planet finds out that there are human women here—capable of having their children—I think there's going to be a rush on trying to nail us down."

"And this, yes, is why I think it is only wise to act now. So, now that you have accepted me as your suitor, I think a short courtship, and we can be married—"

"I haven't accepted you as my suitor."

"But of course you have." His eyes widened. "Oh, pardon me. I have not assured you of the very violence of my attraction to you, have I?"

"Oh. My. Lanta."

"Sorry. That's not translating." He cleared his throat. "It *is* violent. My affection? My attraction? My admiration? And I don't want you to worry, because typically a furnne woman would bring some credits into the situation, and I know you have nothing. But this is no impediment to our union. You don't need to worry about that." He smiled.

He was vile.

"Colle," I said. "I'm going to speak very slowly. I. Do. Not. Want. To. Marry. You. Do you understand?"

He drew back. "What?"

"I don't even want to court you," I said.

He furrowed his brow, which was bushier than Wihke's and not in a pleasant way.

I threw up my hands and left the eating room.

Fannee was there. "Oh, he's asked to be your suitor, then, has he? I told him to. Congratulations to you both."

"No," I said, pushing past her. "I said no."

"She's, um, playing a little game with me," came

Colle's voice, quite amused. "She thinks to refuse a bit and whet my appetite, and I must say it's working."

"Oh snookels," said Fannee, coming after me. "You said no?"

I turned on her. "Fannee, he's... he's..." I just gestured at him, as if this was going to be evident simply by looking at him, which—really—it was.

Fannee tapped her chin with two of her long, blue fingers. "It's because of Wihke. I think you have to forget about him. I don't think he'll be able to come back. I know he was handsome, but..." She leaned in close. "Between you and me, I think this is the only other chance you'll have."

My eyebrows shot up. "There's an entire planet—"

"I've been hearing things," she said, "and it seems that the general consensus amongst those making decisions about you humans is that if the population knew about you, it might cause problems."

"Well, this is the reason they've given for having us locked up here, though, so we aren't raped to death by a stampede of blue men!"

"I suppose they've realized that it must be permanent if they want to make you safe. But they don't want your wombs to go to waste either. There's a thought about artificial insemination—"

"No!" I drew myself up. "What? You're going to keep us here like breeding cows?"

"I don't know what cows are, but—"

"What will happen to our babies?" I whispered.

"Well..." She pressed her lips together.

"Fannee, you can't let this happen."

"I don't know that I have a lot of power, Liz." She gave me a sad look. "But Colle, he has the favor of Her Splendor. If anyone is allowed to marry one of you, it would be him."

I only shook my head in horror.

I went down the hallway to the communicator and I frantically tried to contact Darce. All I got was the out of range message.

I kicked the wall next to it, letting out a string of expletives and curses.

"Liz!"

It was Charlotte.

I turned on her. "Charlotte, we have to get out of here."

"What?"

"It's not going to be like we thought. They're going to artificially inseminate us and make us stay pregnant all the time and take our babies and probably, I don't know, give them to barren furrne women, and we'll be trapped here. What you said, about stealing a ship, about escaping—"

"Liz, we can't *do* any of that. There's no ship. None of us know how to fly it. We can't even drive those tirecraft."

I rested my head against the wall and felt swallowed in despair. This? This would be a good time to cry.

I turned back to the communicator and tried to look for the signature for Wihke's bracelet. I tried to contact it as well. Out of range.

"How do you know this?" she said.

"Colle asked to court me," I said. "I refused. He's awful. But Fannee told me that if I didn't want this other future, he was all I had."

"Of course they all want you." She shook her head at me. "Always the redheads."

"My hair is not red!"

"In the light, it's—"

"My hair is auburn at best, and dishwater brown at the worst. I have frizz and freckles and I'm not even pretty, and—"

"Okay, Liz, okay." She put a hand on my shoulder. "But look at the facts. Darce. Wihke. Colle. Every single man—"

"Not every single man," I said. "Definitely not Darce."

"I'm just saying—"

"What are you saying?"

She let out a breath. "So, you don't want Colle?"

"Of course not."

"How would you feel if I…?"

My lips parted.

"I know," she said. "But listen to me. This is how we do it. We can't get a ship and we can't even get a tirecraft. But I don't mind it. I'll be his wife, and I'll use my position and my influence over him to fix it for you guys."

"While you're having those babies you want that you think fate gave you." I raised my chin and looked her over.

"Do you want to do it?" She raised her chin. "I'll let it be you, since you're the one he wants."

"I could not have sex with that… that…" I felt like gagging. "And the fact that you could—"

"Well, I could," she said. "You know, considering everything, I bet he's a bit trainable, and that's never a bad thing. I think I can make him very, very grateful to me for a number of reasons." She grinned.

I sagged into the wall.

"I will help the rest of you," she said. "It might take time, but this is the way. Trust me. He's so close to the queen or whatever they call her? If I'm his wife? It'll get me close too."

I nodded. "No, I guess you're right. I guess… but I'm sorry you have to do this, Charlotte."

"Nah," she said, giving me a little smile. "It's fate."

"But he's so…" I shuddered. "He's just the worst."

"You think they all have, um, *extras*, though, right?"

"Well, Jane said that Blenge did, so yeah."

"I'll make it work." She winked at me.

And then she sashayed off down the hallway.

I sank down to the floor and buried my face in my hands, wondering whether I should say anything to Jane or Lydia.

NINE

elizabeth

The announcement that Charlotte and Colle would be married came the next morning at breakfast, while we were all gathered around the duplicator. It was pretty obvious that Colle had spent the night in Charlotte's room from the way his uniform looked rumpled and the way he behaved. He could not stop touching her.

He didn't talk very much, though, which was an improvement in my opinion. He let Charlotte share the news, and then he smiled adoringly at her and put his arm around her and sat there smiling like a man who'd just won the lottery or something.

Fannee gave me a look as if to say, *You see what happens when you dally?*

When Colle went out for his guard rotation, we all crowded in Charlotte's room where she announced to us all, perched on her bed, "Virgin. I just corrupted that big, blue alien man thoroughly."

"Well, obviously he was a virgin," I muttered. "Who would want that?"

"Highly trainable, as I said," said Charlotte. "I told him that human women won't even consider intercourse until they've been brought to a climax at least twice and he didn't even blink."

Jane grinned. "Well, Blenge didn't need to be told."

Charlotte grinned back. "And their tongues? Why did no one prepare me for the tongues?"

"Oh, yes," said Jane, sighing.

"Good for kissing," I said.

"Good for *lots* of things," said Charlotte.

Lydia put her hands on her hips. "I don't understand why I'm the only one not to have gone to bed with one of these aliens. Have you *looked* at me?"

"I didn't..." I shrugged. "I mean, Wihke and I didn't go all the way."

"Look at the three of you," said Lydia, "and look at me. I could be a Playmate. I have natural assets and I'm perfectly proportioned —"

"And so humble as well," I said dryly.

She rolled her eyes. "You know what I mean. It's timing, that's what it is. Or maybe I came on too strong with Wihke. I don't know why he was so into you, Liz. What did he say?"

"He said my frizz made me glow in the light." I pointed up to my halo.

"Figures," said Lydia, shaking her head. "Just figures. We go to a planet, and the aliens like the ugly girls."

"Hey," said Jane. "You take that back."

Lydia winced. "I didn't mean it like..." She looked around at us. "Sorry." She sighed. "But *I* would have gone all the way with Wihke."

"We just got interrupted," I said. Of course, that had been kind of a relief, if I was really honest, because it had all been going a little too fast for my liking.

"Anyway, he adores me," said Charlotte. "He worships me. You guys can see that?"

"You made him shut up, I'll give you that," I said.

"He's much less annoying when he's quiet."

"Look, he's…" She smiled, and there was actual affection — genuine affection — in her tone. "He's a little on the ridiculous side sometimes, but deep down, I don't know…" She bit down on her bottom lip. "Trust me when I say that no human man has ever wanted me like that man wanted me." Her voice had gotten a little throaty.

"That's how I felt with Blenge," said Jane. "And then he just disappeared on me."

Charlotte seized her hand. "We don't know what happened with that. Maybe he wants to see you and somehow he's being prevented."

"Who would do that?"

Charlotte looked at me. "You didn't tell them."

I sighed heavily.

"Tell us what?" said Jane.

Charlotte looked at me as if she expected me to start talking. When I didn't, she began to explain it. She quickly added that the plan was for her to marry Colle and use her influence on him to get close to Her Splendor herself, Catte, and get us out of here.

"Well, how long is that going to take?" said Lydia.

"I already told him I want to go to the capital," said Charlotte. "He got really excited and spent twenty minutes telling me about all the things he wants to show me there, and he volunteered the idea of introducing me to the queen. So, hopefully, not long."

"I will not get pregnant with alien babies," said Lydia.

"That's like the reason they brought us here," said Charlotte.

"Well, I at least want sex first. I at least want these tongues you guys are all raving about." Lydia glared at us with pure rancor.

"Guys," I said, "we definitely can't be kept here as breeding stock, but I don't know what the alternative is. Charlotte, are you going to be safe in the capital?"

"Why wouldn't I be?"

"Because when men see that Colle has you, of all people, what's going to stop them from trying to take you from him?" I said.

She went still, thinking about this. "Well, I'm sure that won't happen. It's not as if these aliens aren't civilized."

"They have no women," I said. "You don't think they're going to be desperate?"

"I'm sure Colle is under royal protection," said Charlotte.

I nodded slowly. "Yeah, I guess so. But the rest of us? If we're not breeding machines—"

"We need powerful husbands," said Charlotte. "Men who have the resources and status and connections to protect us, that's all."

Lydia snorted. "And you guys said that I was setting the women's movement back twenty years."

"There is no women's movement in space," snapped Jane.

"But you guys are like, 'Well, we need to screw powerful men so that they'll protect us!'" Lydia snorted at us. "I'll find some other way, thank you."

"Like what?" I said.

"Well, I'm going to get Forste to teach me to use a blaster. That's what they call their guns."

"We all have translators, Lydia," muttered Charlotte.

"You know what? I'm bored with this conversation," said Lydia, standing up. "And with all of you as well." She swept out of the room and the door slid closed in her wake.

We all sat in silence, staring after her for several minutes.

I looked at Charlotte. "Can you get Colle to teach you how to drive a tirecraft?"

"Definitely," she said. She squared her shoulders. "And if Darce comes back—"

"Darce does not like me," I said.

"He's never spoken to *me* alone," said Jane.

"He hates human women!" I looked back and forth between them both.

"So, why did he take us from the Toth ship?" said Charlotte.

I shrugged. "I don't know."

"I'm only saying—"

"Both of you are crazy," I said. "Like you said, you've never talked to him alone. I have. And he is not into humans at all and definitely not me. I promise you that."

"But if he was, you'd use that to help us," said Charlotte.

I straightened up. "Pretend to be into him to manipulate him, you mean?" *Anything that smacks of cunning disgusts you.*

"Hmm." Charlotte nodded. "So, you're fine with it if I'm doing it, but if you did it, it would be unthinkable."

I looked away, sighing.

"We don't owe them anything," said Jane. "Blenge used me. He just wanted to experience the oddity of sex with a human. Put a notch on his belt. He can brag to the other furrne men about how he got me out of my panties in two seconds flat."

I nodded. "If I could manipulate him, then I would. Yes."

"Okay," said Charlotte.

"But it won't ever come to that," I said. "And besides, I don't know if he'll ever come back here."

Pleiccs passed and the marriage of Charlotte and Colle was performed. According to Fannee, the ceremony would usually be very elaborate and involve pleiccs and neicchs of feasting and a big party. But we just had duplicator spaghetti rings and they stood up in front of all of us and promised something that was a lot like forsaking all others and till death do us part, but in alien words.

And then, two pleiccs later, they left for the capital, and another guard came to replace Colle. We really had the turnover rate with guards, it seemed.

This guy's name was Denne, and Lydia lost no time in trying out his tongue. And the rest of him, too, I suppose. Whenever he wasn't on duty, he was either in Lydia's room or sitting around with Lydia on his lap as she cooed to him. He let her braid his hair and he did most of his talking to her cleavage, which she always showed off now. She'd altered all of her clothes to do that, creating deep Vs in every single shirt. The talking he did—well, it wasn't much, admittedly.

Lydia didn't talk much to the rest of us, since she spent her time either in Denne's lap or with Forste's wife (whose name I didn't even know). A couple times, though, either Jane or I would get her to talk and she said that Denne didn't know anything about a breeding program and that he said he *would* marry Lydia, but that he wasn't allowed. Only Colle had been given that permission, it seemed.

We got messages from Charlotte now and again from the capital, but she said she was kept hidden a lot of the time, and that she was sneaked in and out of the royal castle when Colle dined with Her Splendor Catte, and that there was never any real chance for her to say anything, because the two of them chatted back and forth with each other and she couldn't get a word in edgewise.

However, she said that she was dropping hints to Colle that she was lonely and wished to see us, and that she was working on getting him to speak to Her Splendor about it. She was determined to derail the breeding plan, and she wouldn't stop until she'd accomplished that.

Colle loves me and he wants to please me, Charlotte's voice said on the recording. *He'll help us. I know he will.*

I wished that I was as confident.

One day, there was a message from Darce for Jane, Lydia, and me. He presented to us the idea of being breeding stock, but he acted like it was a better option for us than anything else, saying that our presence would drive the men on the planet mad, and this would keep us safe. He said that he'd make sure that any of us who wanted to keep one of our children for companionship would be allowed, as if this was some kind of grand favor.

Well, so much for Charlotte being able to stop it! It was going forward, and here was the proof.

I tried to send a message back, but there was no way to do so.

He said he wouldn't do anything without our consent, but that if we weren't earning our keep in one way, we might need to be employed some other way, and this shocked me. How dare he?

Since we were going to have to consent, I assumed we'd get a chance to say our piece, and when that happened, I was going to rip him a new one.

That man.

He made me furious.

Jane was not angry, only terrified, and Lydia redoubled her efforts with Denne.

I wanted to find some way to leave, and we did have access to what they called the networks, but all of it was written in languages we couldn't read.

I asked Fannee if there were some resources we could use to learn to read it, like maybe what they gave to children. I tried to ask if the letters were phonetically rendered or if the characters pictorially represented whole concepts. She was disturbingly evasive, however, and she eventually confessed to me that she'd been told it would be better if we didn't learn to read.

Why was that, I wondered?

Maybe then we'd be able to discover that treating us the way they were treating us violated their laws or something, I bet.

I hated Darce.

I fantasized about punching him until his nose bled.

But it wasn't Darce who woke me up in the middle of the night, six blue fingers over my mouth cautioning me to be quiet.

No, it was Wihke.

I struggled, then realized it was him and went still.

He slowly removed his fingers.

"What are you doing here?" I said.

He kissed me.

I let him. It even felt good. But when he started deepening the kiss and getting more intense with his tongue, I pulled away. "How did you get in?"

"I have my ways," he said. "I maybe called in a favor with Denne. I needed to see you. I can't stop thinking about you. I want to look at you, Liz. I want to see every part of you and I want to put my mouth—"

"Okay, sure," I said. "But not right now. We need your help. You have to get us out of here."

He furrowed his brow. "What's going on?"

I explained to him about Darce's offer, about how we'd be kept pregnant and how they'd take our children, and how Darce had the gall to say this was being done for our safety.

He sneered. "That sounds like something Darce would try to do."

"It's wrong," I said. "It's evil and it's a violation of basic rights." I swallowed. Okay, I wasn't good with this manipulation thing, but... I leaned into him, running my fingers over his firm chest and made my voice breathy. "If you really want to put your mouth all over me, Wihke, you'll get me out of here."

He drew back, looking at me with very serious eyes. "Okay."

"Okay?" I let out a shaky breath. "And Jane and Lydia too."

He furrowed his brow. "That's going to make it so much harder, Liz." He twined a strand of my hair around one of his blue fingers. "I can't tonight. I don't even have room enough in the single speeder I brought for you, let alone all three of you."

I pressed into him, keeping that breathy voice that I hoped was actually sexy. I wasn't really good at this, I didn't think. "You can do it. I know you can."

"Yeah, I'll come back for you," he said, his voice stronger, more confident. "I'll get all three of you. I promise. I'll take you somewhere safe, and no one will ever find you."

I kissed him.

He kissed back, aggressive, pushing his body into

mine, and now we were horizontal on my bed, his body over mine.

I gasped, surprised. "Wihke—"

"For this neicch, though, Liz, let's make each other forget about all of that. Let's just lose ourselves in each other? You are all I think about." He kissed my jaw, and then under my jaw, a hint of his agile tongue, and goosebumps puckered all over my skin, and I let out another gasp. "You have no idea how badly I want you."

I actually might have an idea, because I could feel his erection pressing into me, and his tongue was doing crazy things to me, moving against the sensitive spots on my neck, making me feel shivery, and yet—

"Stop," I said to him.

He didn't.

"Wihke." I was out of breath, practically panting.

"Liz," he groaned into my skin. His tongue found my clavicle, and now he was cupping one of my breasts, squeezing it through my nightclothes. I wasn't wearing one of the supporters to sleep in, even if I had to admit the bust supporters were definitely more comfortable than Earth bras. Even so, nothing was inducing me to sleep in one. He pinched the tip of my breast—too hard.

It hurt. I let out a noise of protest. "Seriously, Wihke. I mean it, stop."

He went still, but he didn't move off me. "I'm sorry, Liz. I just lose control when I'm—"

"Well, get control back," I said, and I was afraid.

He pushed up on his arms over me. "Hey," he said. "What's that about?"

I swallowed. *Don't make him angry. You need him. If you have to sleep with him to get him to free you, then do it,* because that's how manipulation works. "Nothing."

He furrowed his brow. "When we were together before, I know you wanted this as much as I did."

"I..." I tried to smile. "I do. I guess I'm just scared of being trapped here and turned into a breeding animal or something, you know? It's hard to feel in the mood when that's all I can think about?"

He eyed me. "Oh."

"But, um..." I drew in a breath. Tell him to continue. Touch him. Do something.

But I was completely still and quiet, just looking up at him, and I couldn't force myself to do anything at all. I was simply frozen. I wanted to cry in frustration and confusion, and the thing was? At that moment, I didn't want Wihke to touch me at all. His weight on me was actually terrifying, and I felt imprisoned under his huge frame.

He sat up and looked me over. "Maybe I was going too fast. Sorry. I've been imagining this for too long, and I got overly eager. We'll slow down."

"Good," I whispered. I wanted him to leave. I didn't know why. It didn't even make sense, but I felt panicked right now.

He reached out with his long blue fingers, all six of them, and he ran them over my nightclothes, starting at my clavicle, between my breasts, all the way down my body to my belly button.

I shivered again, but it wasn't a totally good shiver. I didn't get this. I couldn't really be frightened of Wihke. He was gorgeous and charming and interested in me, and he was my suitor, and... and it must be what I'd said. It must be the thoughts of the threat of being artificially inseminated, always pregnant, used like that. Because I knew I liked Wihke.

He leaned down over me, his long dark hair falling down around his face. His voice was soft. "The thing is, I have to go soon, Liz. Maybe… you think you could touch me like before?" His hand found one of mine and pressed it into his hardness. "You make me so crazy, I won't last any time at all."

I curved my hand around him through his clothes. "Sure." My voice was too high-pitched.

He kissed me again. While he did it, he worked at his pants, freeing himself, and then I was stroking him again, like I had last time. His thick, hot hardness was in my hand and I rubbed him as he kissed me.

It… I still felt panicked, but he seemed into it. He sighed into my mouth, whispering my name in an affected voice, and it didn't last that long.

His semen was mostly like a human's, except it seemed like there was a lot of it, and it was all over my hand and a little bit of it was on my nightclothes and the sheets, and it… I…

But he just kissed me and tucked himself away and said he'd come back for me, for all of us, and then he left the room.

I lay there, his ejaculate cooling on my hand, feeling used and disgusting and on the verge of tears.

Stupid, Elizabeth, I told myself firmly. *There's no reason to be like this. You should have let him have sex with you.*

Then I got up and went to the wasteroom down the hall and cleaned my hand and my nightclothes and I went back to bed, and the room smelled like sex, and my nightclothes were wet and there was a spot on the bed that I had to roll away from and I didn't even know how I was going to clean it or if I'd get in trouble if anyone knew that Wihke had been there…

I didn't get back to sleep for a long time.

TEN

"They've refused," I said to my aunt, holder of the high seat of our planet. She was seated in her audience room and I was standing in front of her, my hands clasped behind my back.

"What do you mean? I never said to give them a choice." My aunt Catte sniffed.

"When I rescued them from the Toth, I promised them they'd never have to do anything they didn't wish to do," I said to her.

She sniffed again.

I actually felt pretty awful about even offering it at this point. I'd spoken to Elizabeth, who'd given me quite a verbal lashing, falling into human words that I didn't understand here and there, my translator sometimes flashing in my brain *possible expletive*, and she'd made it clear to me that she and the others would never wish to participate in such a thing and that she found the idea of it despicable.

I supposed I'd been fooling myself that there was any way to see it otherwise. I had spun it in odd ways in my head—perhaps they were frightened of sexual intercourse with us and this spared them that—or perhaps they *would* feel safer this way.

But I could no longer deceive myself into thinking

there were any merits to the idea.

"You'll have to break your promise," she said.

"I won't," I said. "I'm now opposed to the entire proposition."

"You most certainly are not," she said. "You can't be. This is a lesson you'll have to learn, nephew, before you take over the high seat of the planet, and that is that you can't allow morals to get in the way of ruling."

"Well, how can one rule without morals, Your Splendor? With respect, I mean." I lowered my gaze on the last bit.

"It's a question of which is the larger evil," she said. "And in this case, we need their wombs. It's for the good of the planet."

"No, there's not enough of them to truly make a difference." What Blenge had said? It had stuck with me, and the more I thought it through, the more I realized it was true. "How many children could they each possibly even have? There are only three left. Even assuming that they could have one child a year and that their bodies wouldn't give out, the maximum is probably twenty, and that would be… horrific." I thought of Elizabeth's body wasted and worn out, but I refused to let any emotion work its way into my voice, because my aunt wouldn't care. She would only term it weakness on my part. "But what is sixty children for an entire planet, Your Splendor? Not nearly enough."

"It's better than none," she said primly.

"Besides, the genetics don't work," I said. "They'd be siblings."

"Not all of them. The girls themselves are not related at all. As long as they did not breed with siblings—"

"Even so, there's not enough of them, and within several generations, they would all be intermingled."

"I've run careful scenarios, and I think it can be worked around," she said.

I shook my head. "We'd put these sixty children into the nobility, I suppose."

"Naturally."

"And then the lower class would revolt and kill us all," I said.

"No, they would recognize the new generation must have the best of everything and would want them to be raised in comfort."

"And when this generation is gone, and the next comes of age, and the lower classes have had no children, who will serve this fledgling nobility, all that is left of the planet, a group of pampered beings with no skills?"

"What is the alternative, Darce? To watch everyone die? This is hope, some kind of hope."

"I don't know," I muttered. And I didn't. "Maybe there really is no hope, Your Splendor."

"I refuse to accept that," she said. "And I'm removing you from this project."

"What do you mean?"

"I'm going to do it," she said. "Those human women will be bred. You don't have to be part of it if you're too squeamish."

"You can't do that," I said.

"I hold the high seat of the planet Plembe. I am Her Splendor, Catte. I can do whatever it is that I please." She lifted her chin and looked down her nose at me.

This was not precisely true, as her power was limited by our elected council houses, like a senate, but this project was not known to the government, so I couldn't use them to wrest power from her.

No, if I was going to do anything, I'd have to use the

secretive nature of it all against her.

* * *

elizabeth

Wihke didn't return.

Two-ten mooncrosses came and went, and he didn't come back. I asked Denne about it, and he said that he'd only offered Wihke a one-shot deal to come in, and that, as far as he knew, Wihke had no plans of returning.

I told myself that he hadn't known I'd needed rescuing, but then I wondered what his intention had been to come in the first place, if he'd known it was only once.

Maybe he'd just come to try to get between my thighs.

Immediately, I told myself it wasn't true, that there were men who behaved that way, but Wihke couldn't be one of them. That he wasn't nearly so awful nor so idiotic. It must mean more to him if he took the risk of getting caught to get to me. Who would risk that much just for, well, what turned out to be a hand job?

Which he'd been pretty insistent on getting, though.

No.

I could trust Wihke. He was coming back. We would all get out of here.

I told myself that over and over, but time kept passing, and he didn't come back.

One night, I awoke to the sound of my door opening.

I recognized the furrne man who stood in the doorway, Lydia and Jane behind him, huddled in their nightclothes. It was Rehke, the other of the three men who'd taken us from the Toth ship.

"Quiet," he said in a low voice. "Come with me now."

I got out of bed. "Come with you where?"

"Somewhere else," he said. "Where you won't be turned into breeding receptacles. That's all I can tell you."

I hurried over to him.

"Stay behind me," he said to us. "Stay close to each other." He brandished his blaster and took a step forward.

Jane clasped my hand. Lydia bit down on her bottom lip. "What about Denne? I feel like he—"

"Lydia, if you want to stay here," I said, "then by all means, go screaming to Denne. But you asked him for help, didn't you?"

"Quiet," said Rehke.

We fell silent.

He motioned for us to follow him, and we all moved quickly and quietly down the corridor.

At the end, he stopped and we stopped too.

He peered out, looking one way and then the other, sighting the area with his blaster. Gesturing to us that it was safe, we all stepped out and started toward the back door.

Suddenly, Forste appeared, holding his blaster. When he saw it was Rehke, he hesitated.

Rehke pointed his blaster at Forste. "I'd hate to shoot you."

"Both of us might get shot." Forste gestured with his blaster. "What's going on?"

"You got the orders coming down from the high seat?" said Rehke. "What they're going to do to them?"

Forste flinched.

"You know it's wrong," said Rehke. "And there's only three of them. It's not even worth it. It won't save the planet."

The tip of Forste's blaster wavered. Abruptly, he pulled it back, pointing it at the floor. "I never saw you. You never saw me. This never happened."

"Never did," said Rehke in acknowledgment, lowering his blaster.

Forste walked past us, letting us go.

Rehke ushered us out of the building and into a waiting tirecraft. There were furs inside and we huddled into them against the cold, the three of us women on one side and Rehke facing us. Someone else was driving the tirecraft, and it took off.

Rehke set his blaster down on the seat next to him and eyed us.

"Thank you," I whispered.

"You're Elizabeth, right?" he said, looking me over.

"That's right," I said.

"You're coming to the capital with me," he said.

"What?" I said. "Why?"

Rehke looked at the other girls. "The two of you, you'll be hidden elsewhere, somewhere safe."

"You're separating us?" said Jane.

"Why is Elizabeth going to the capital?" said Lydia. "Why do all the men on this planet want Elizabeth?"

"I'm not—" Rehke cleared his throat. "She's not for me." And then he gave me a completely different look, an appraising, male sort of look, and—in spite of myself—my stomach flipped over. "Not that you're not very attractive," he said to me. "No offense meant."

"None taken," I said quietly. "But I don't understand."

"There's a plan," he said. "It's dangerous and knowing what we know of you, we thought you'd be the one who'd be willing to undertake it. You're the one who insisted on going after Jane and who showed no compunction in screaming your refusal into Darce's face, after all. There are very few people on the planet who'd talk to him that way."

I flushed. "I just—"

"No, it's good," he said. "You're brave. This will require bravery."

"What do I have to do?"

"Liz, you don't have to do anything you don't want to do," said Jane, squeezing my hand. "Why does she have to be in danger?"

"To save all of you," said Rehke.

"How?" said Lydia. "Not that I'm volunteering or anything because I'm not. Not for danger."

"There are a lot of moving parts," he said. "All will be explained. I'm the one who came for you because I have a high rank in the planetary army, and my security clearance allows me to get in pretty much anywhere. But rest assured, my aunt is not going to be happy this has happened. Not at all."

"You can't just volunteer Liz," said Jane.

"Well, I didn't," he said with a smirk.

"So, who did?" I said.

"Darce, of course."

ELEVEN

"This is all very irregular," Colle was saying. "Elizabeth arrived in the middle of the neicch, and my instinct was to tell Her Splendor, but I had to· admit that I didn't know if I should wake her, and it did seem quite a bother to get dressed and set off all the way across to the palace, so I opted to do it first thing, which I would be doing right now if you were not here, right inside my doorway, at a very unreasonable time, I might add."

I was standing just inside the foyer of Colle's town house, which was a modest house as befit a man who worked for the royal regiment. He was now in the private service of my aunt, and worked on a rotation to guard her within the palace.

"I do want you to tell my aunt that she's here," I said. "Of course I do. Just not quite yet."

"Not yet?" Colle folded his arms over his chest. "Well, what could possibly induce me to delay?"

"Me, of course," I said. "That's why I'm here." I pulled up my bracelet. "And I did tell others to be here right about now, but they're—"

There was an entry query at the front door.

"Ah," I said, turning and palming the controls so that the door opened.

In came a royal dressmaker with a wardrobe of ready-made dresses. I'd gotten access to Elizabeth's measurements from when they'd been taken when clothes were procured for her before, and these dresses should hopefully fit. It was just a question of which one she should wear this pleicc.

Colle sputtered. "You can't let people into my house!"

"Oh?" I said. "But I have."

"Listen, of all of the humans to be here, the one that I wish least to host is the one who refused to allow me to court her! She has to go. And when I tell Her Splendor…"

But I didn't hear what he'd said because his voice trailed off as I motioned for the dressmaker to accompany me into the house.

Colle's voice roared back to life as he pursued me. "Where are you going?"

"You said she was at breakfast with your wife, didn't you?"

"Well, I could hardly deny my sweet Charlotte the chance to reconnect with her friend," said Colle. "Charlotte is a most excellent choice, and even Catte agrees with me that I have a most excellent wife."

I glanced at him over my shoulder. "My aunt likes you. Ice gods only know why, but she does. That's why you'll present her."

"Present whom?"

"Elizabeth," I said. I pointed. "Is this the dining room here?"

"You cannot simply barge into my house and bring dresses and—" Colle threw up his hands. "I don't care if you *are* the heir. This is highly irregular!"

I palmed the controls and the door to the dining

room slid open and there she was.

She stood up, her eyes wide, her face turning red and changing the color of her freckles. Her hair was smoothed back at the nape of her neck, but little pieces of it had come free all around her head, and I found myself wanting—

Well, none of that.

"Lovely to see you again, Elizabeth," I said.

"Darce," she said in a tight voice. "Rehke said you wanted me here, and he said there was a plan, and I don't suppose you're going to share it with me any time soon?"

"This... this..." Colle sputtered again, in the doorway, and then someone who was carrying a dress smacked into him and knocked him sideways, and he stumbled, crying out, fumbling to catch himself. "I won't *stand* for this."

I went over to him, taking him by the arm and righting him.

He pulled away, slapping at my hands. "Don't you touch me." He busied himself brushing at his uniform, picking at invisible bits of lint.

"Take Elizabeth and your wife to the public presentation this pleicc."

Colle turned on me with a horrified expression. "But no one is to blanic know about the humans."

"Exactly," I said. "That's what we have to change."

"I... I *won't*." He squared his shoulders. "Absolutely not. Catte would be angry with me."

"I don't think she will," I said. I smiled at him. "You're so very brint with her, after all. She does favor you so."

"This will end her favor for me, and I hesitate to—"

"You'll think of something to say," I said, shrugging.

"I've seen you with her. She eats up whatever comes from your mouth. It's frankly puzzling to me, but it's undeniable."

"But what could possibly induce me to do such a thing?" He glared at me.

"You're aware of Catte's plan for the other human women?" I said.

"Well, yes, I suppose," he said.

"You think that once the entire planet is aware of the human women's existence, that they'll allow you to keep your wife here and not insist that she become part of the breeding group?"

"No one is supposed to know—"

"You can do it," I said. "You can present Charlotte and Elizabeth publicly to Her Splendor, or I can break the news elsewhere, but everyone on the planet is going to know one way or the other. If you do this, you'll have some control over Her Splendor. If you don't, well, it will all be in my hands."

"Darce," said Elizabeth. "If everyone knows about us, then… it won't be safe."

I glanced at her. "I thought Rehke explained to you this was dangerous."

Her lips parted.

"Not to worry, Rehke is well-liked," I said. "I'm sure we can count on some members of the planetary army to disobey orders from the high seat and do as he says."

Elizabeth gasped.

I turned on Colle. "Or, of course, Colle could convince Catte to give the orders to protect you herself."

Colle had turned a pale shade of greenish blue. His lips trembled and so did his hands. "You… you…." He could not seem to finish his sentence, but I could see that he was staring at me with deep hatred.

"You wouldn't let anything happen to your sweet Charlotte," I said. "Would you?"

"This doesn't make any sense," said Elizabeth. "Why would you put us in danger? This whole time, you've insisted that it has to be a secret—"

"Because I believe in my people," I said. "You know, we all kept saying that if the men on this planet knew you existed, they'd go mad, but of all the men who did know, were any one of you actually molested?" I didn't wait very long. "No. Everyone who knew behaved honorably. You were not hurt. So, I believe that if I tell them to control themselves, they will."

"But what if they don't?" This was from Charlotte.

"Well, that's why your husband will secure protection from the high seat." I turned to him.

"I despise you," he said.

"I'd gathered," I said. "But you'll do it."

"I don't have a choice," he said.

"You really don't," I said. "And now, we don't have a lot of time, so we'll need to decide on dresses." I gestured for the dressmaker, who begun to unzip garment bags and pull things out.

"This is all wrong," said Colle. "You've brought such fancy clothes. You're dressing her up like royalty."

"I'm dressing her in formal clothing, which is what anyone would wear for an audience with Her Splendor," I said.

"What will please Her Splendor is if we come before her humbly as befits our station," said Colle. "Isn't that right, Charlotte darling? When we dine with her, we only wear as best as we have, and she has often commented on how it is gratifying to her that she has raised you to such a position?"

Charlotte made a face. "I do think she enjoys feeling her, er, lofty station in life."

I sighed.

"I didn't mean it to sound…" Charlotte turned to her husband. "Darling, you know that I—"

"You were quite exactly right in describing her," said Colle to her. "Indeed, she is lofty, and she has been quite good to us, hasn't she? We *are* below her. It is as it should be to confirm all that."

I turned to the dressmaker. "Did you bring anything… plainer?"

The dressmaker sorted through her garment bags and pulled something out. It was brown, made of soft suede-like material with white fur fringes at the sleeves and hem. It was based on traditional garb of our planet. It was respectful but humble.

"That would work," said Colle.

"Fine, then," I said.

Elizabeth looked back and forth between me and Charlotte and the dress. "I'm so confused right now."

* * *

elizabeth

Darce was gone in as much of a flurry as he'd arrived. He'd barely looked at me, and when he did, his expression had been even more of an appraisal and evaluation than ever, and I felt even more as though I was coming up wanting. Why did he always seem to dismiss me?

He had barely spoken to me, and I wondered if it was because he was in some kind of a snit at having to follow Rehke's plan. At least, I assumed it was Rehke's plan. I couldn't make heads or tails of it, which was probably because he hadn't explained it to me!

But now, here I was dressed up in this long dress

with fur-edged sleeves and hems—which was actually very soft and comfortable, and Charlotte was dressed too, and Colle was fuming as he herded us into the tirecraft.

I had gathered that we were going to be presented to Her Splendor, and that the plan somehow involved the entire planet knowing about our existence. I wasn't entirely sure why that was the plan or what was supposed to be accomplished by doing it.

I might have thought about it and maybe figured out some sort of advantage to the reveal, but I hadn't had a chance to do anything. We hadn't even finished breakfast—my first breakfast on the planet that hadn't come from a duplicator, in fact, which I'd been pretty curious about. I'd been put in this dress and my hair had been first brushed out and then—when the servant realized exactly what happened to my hair after brushing (it got frizzier and poofier)—sleeked back again into a bun.

Colle kept up a steady monologue the whole time in the tirecraft, worrying over what it was that he could possibly say to Her Splendor, talking about what would happen if she decided to dismiss him from her service and vowing that he would do everything in his power to save Charlotte, who looked pale and concerned and kept twisting her hands together in the middle of her lap.

Maybe it was a good thing I hadn't had the rest of my breakfast.

I was starting to feel nauseated.

Eventually, the tirecraft stopped and we got out. We moved through the frigid air for only a few feet before entering into an arched doorway, where it was warm. Then we emerged into a vast room—huge, the size of a stadium, though there weren't graduated seats. Instead, there were crowds of people on either side of the large room, and the air buzzed with conversation.

Colle propelled us both in front of him and went to a furnne man in a dark uniform. "We'd like to be placed on the docket to see Her Splendor."

The man looked us over, eyes wide. "What are…? They're not Toth, but they look—"

"Humans," said Colle. "From the wormhole."

"*Oh.*" The man openly gaped at us in wonder. "I'll move you to the front of the list, then."

Colle cringed. "Thank you," he said in a strangled voice.

We moved away from the man and Colle's face turned darker blue, almost green, and he muttered to himself and smoothed out his clothes and fidgeted and shook off Charlotte when she tried to soothe him.

Charlotte had been stunned to see me when Rehke had dropped me off at their house the night before, but she'd also been welcoming and pleased, hugging me so hard that she'd practically cracked my ribs. Now, she just looked terrified, however.

A hush came over the crowd.

Some horned instruments blew at the front of the room and some drums were struck.

Then all of the people in the room lifted their hands and began rubbing their fingers together, a soft sort of whispering noise that I thought might be something like applause in our culture.

Into this stepped Her Splendor, Catte, the holder of the high seat of Plembe—which was how a crier described her as she settled onto a chair at the top of a raised dais.

The finger rubbing stopped.

Catte cleared her throat. "My people," she said, her voice amplified somehow. They must have something like microphones here. "It is so brint to be among you for the public presentation. I know there was some concern we would not hold the ceremony this year, since there are so few of our daughters remaining and coming of age, but I felt that we must keep our traditions strong!"

More finger rubbing. The drums were struck in a volley.

"Who is first on the docket?" she said.

And then Colle's name was called, along with mine and Charlotte's.

The room went entirely silent, and Colle offered his arms to both of us.

We curved our hands on his elbows and we walked to the front of the room, between all of those who were gathered there, all the way to the front of the room, to the dais, where the man in the black uniform, who we'd spoken to before, handed Colle a small silvery thing, like a brooch. He pinned it on his shirt and cleared his throat, and I realized it was a microphone, or whatever they might call that here.

Now, I could see Catte better, since we were closer, and Her Splendor was blue and regal, her dark hair woven into a towering braided creation on her head. Her face was lined and severe. Her lips were thin, but they had been painted a deep purple color and she was gripping the arms of her chair with the six fingers on each of her hands.

She did not look happy.

Colle opened his mouth and then closed it.

Catte's nostrils flared. Her lips thinned even more.

"Your Splendor," said Colle. His voice was

trembling. "You need no introduction to my wife, of course, because you have dined with her on a number of occasions."

Catte straightened, letting out a breath that her microphone picked up. Her expression was lethal.

"This is one of the other humans who you freed from the Toth, one Elizabeth Bennet," asid Colle. "Both my wife and Elizabeth wished to thank you for their freedom in person. This is why I have brought them here to you." He glanced at us meaningfully.

We didn't know what to do.

Catte herself looked even angrier.

Colle's voice was still shaking. "They wish to touch their foreheads in supplication and respect."

Oh, okay?

Colle did it, and Charlotte and I both followed suit.

"The Toth are stealing human women to use as breeding stock," said Colle, his voice strengthening. "But you, in your wisdom, rescued a few of them—the ones you could save—because you know, Your Splendor, that we are nothing like the Toth."

The room erupted in finger rubbing abruptly.

"You are so good, Your Splendor," said Colle. "So very, very good to have done this." Abruptly, he put a hand over his microphone and ran for the dais.

Catte pointed to her microphone, which I could see now, pinned to her dress, and then leaned forward.

Colle and Catte put their heads close, conversing in low voices for some time until she straightened up and patted him on the cheek sympathetically and then motioned for him to go back down.

Catte pointed to her microphone again.

When she spoke, her voice filled the room. "My people, I was surprised to see these lovely human women here, because I understood they were frightened and wished for their presence here to be kept secret, but I am pleased to announce that they are here, and that we have rescued them from the Toth, and of course I am here to accept their thanks, poor homeless refugees who take shelter here with us." She bowed to us. Then she motioned with one hand and two men in regiment uniforms, like the ones we'd seen on the men who guarded us, came and ushered Colle, Charlotte, and me away.

We were shut up in a small room where we could hear the echoes of Catte's amplified voice from time to time, but couldn't quite make it out.

Colle told us that he'd told her that he'd been forced into it by Darce, and that Catte had been immediately forgiving at that point.

I wasn't sure if that was good. Would that ruin the plan? *What* was the plan?

Sometime later, the door to the small room opened and Her Splendor stood there, looking us all over disapprovingly.

"Well, Colle, this is all a disaster," said Catte.

"I am so sorry, Your Splendor." He hurried over to her. "I was… he threatened my Charlotte, and you and I have both agreed how she was such a brint choice."

"Yes, indeed, Colle," said Catte. "Your wife is quite a credit to you." She turned on me. "This one, though. Elizabeth, is it?"

I nodded.

"Who brought you to the capital?"

I swallowed.

"Answer me, girl," said Catte.

I wasn't sure if I should or not, but if they'd wanted me to do things right, they should have shared the plan with me. "Rehke of the clan Firne," I said in a very small voice.

"My own nephews," said Catte, shaking her head. "I should have known all of you men would have your heads turned by these girls." She sighed. "Well, nothing for it now, I'm afraid. Now, Elizabeth, tell me where the others are."

"The others?" I said.

"The other girls."

"I-I don't know," I said. "Rehke said it was better if I didn't know, so that I couldn't, um, tell anyone."

"Yes, quite clever," muttered Catte. "What is he trying to accomplish?" She turned to Colle. "Did he tell you to announce to everyone that the Toth are stealing human women?"

"N-no, Your Splendor. He left it entirely up to me, but I could not think, and I was so very terrified, and I never wish to go against your orders or desires, and you can't know how much this has pained me and how much—"

"Oh, there, there, Colle." She lifted a hand. "I do know." Her voice had grown softer, sympathetic. "It's all right. I could not turn against my Colle, never fear."

"You are too good to me." Colle was wiping at tears.

"Just good enough," she said affectionately. Then she looked at me and her expression went severe again. "Well. They all know about you now. We'll simply have to deal with it. I'll speak to you over dinner this neicch, then. All three of you. Do make sure you're on time."

"We are always on time, Your Splendor," said Colle.

She gave him an indulgent smile and then glared at me and then exited the room.

* * *

I looked up from the holoprojection on my bracelet. I was in my town house, in my study, and my cousin Rehke had just arrived.

"This plan of yours," he said. "Are you making it up as you go along?"

"No, no," I said. "I have it planned out in detail. Excruciating detail."

He snorted. "I don't know if I share your high opinion of yourself, cousin. But thus far, it's gone all right, and our aunt has installed extra security on Colle's house. Elizabeth can remain there for now. Aunt Catte seems to think it's better if both human women are in one spot."

"I thought she would," I said. "And have there been any issues thus far?"

"Two attempts to get in," he said.

"That many?" I sighed.

"I would have thought more, personally," he said.

"Well, I said something about believing the best of the men of our species, some nonsense about honor, but I suppose that all goes out the window when a man is, er, frustrated enough."

"We're going to make an example of them," he said. "Public trials, throw the book at them—"

"No," I said. "No, I want it hidden, and I want the official word from the regiment to be how pleased we are at the honorable and civilized manner with which our people are conducting themselves."

He raised his eyebrows. "Truly?"

"Something Her Splendor said to me about morality," I muttered. "Anyway, this is not what I wished to speak to you about." I jammed my finger into the middle of the holoprojection, which was a rendering of ships in space.

"Right," he said, coming around to stand next to me and peer at the projection himself. "What am I looking at? Is this a Toth ship?"

"Coming out of the wormhole," I said. "I scanned and its manifest has it docking at the space station in the Finner Sector for a planned time of three gemoons."

"Why would they do that?" said Rehke, furrowing his brow.

"I don't know. Perhaps it takes time to subdue the human women? Or perhaps they're holding them back, creating artificial scarcity amongst the Toth nobility that are likely bidding on them?"

"That's possible," he said, rubbing his finger over his chin.

I turned to him. "Could we do it?"

He raised his eyebrows. "You mean, take the women?"

"If the scans I conducted are correct, there are hundreds of them aboard that ship. You know that's enough to make a difference here. It's not enough for every single man, of course, but it's enough to save the species."

He squared his shoulders. "I don't know, Darce, does it really fix anything?"

"How could you say that?"

"I'm only saying, as you're pointing out, it's not enough for every single man on the planet, so we're still going to have riots and violence and a number of other issues, and it'll be worse, because once we do this, we're cut off from the rest of the galaxy. The Toth would never forgive us. They might not be able to get through the lectre field and hurt us, but if anyone ever leaves this planet again, they'd be executed immediately. Not to mention, all the trade—"

"We'll build more greenhouses. Food is all that matters, truly. We already provide all our own fuel. Anyway, we won't be going off planet anymore."

"I don't know if the people on the planet are going to agree with you that food is all that matters," he said. "Telling people they can't leave, that their lives will be forfeit if they try to visit the rest of the galaxy? That's not going to go over well."

"That's a small portion of the population," I said. "It's only the nobility who even have the capability to fly off on their own ships."

"They're the ones who will complain the loudest anyway."

"But they are a smaller number compared to the lower class, which is more populous."

"But they can raise militia—"

"You're not answering my question, Rehke. Can we get the ship?"

"Why?"

"I think it's obvious why. I'm trying to save our species from dying out."

"Yes, you and Aunt Catte keep acting as though we won't simply go off to other planets and meet women of other species and bring them back here. As if that's somehow not an option you've even considered."

"You and Aunt Catte keep acting as though the entire planet is only made up of rich people, as if the rest of the planet doesn't matter."

"That's not true. And doing this is a permanent move, Darce."

I repeated my question. "*Can* we do it?"

"You mean, can our forces handle an operation like that? Can we take the space station and commandeer a ship? Yes, absolutely. We can do it with minimal casualties and quickly, and I know just the squadron to put on the job."

I let out a breath.

"But you still haven't explained to me why," he said.

"I *have.*"

He only glared at me.

"Rehke, the Toth have all gone mad. The entire species has. Maybe they were always mad, and we didn't notice because they were fighting too much amongst themselves. But now, they've turned their madness outwards, and their malevolence is concerning. I'm not convinced the Toth will allow us to repopulate our planet. I've seen what's been happening in the galactic senate, and it's very concerning. You know that there are now Toth representatives for seven planets, planets where very few Toth even live?"

"That's not what it's about, Darce," he said. "Are you lying to me or to yourself?"

"What are you talking about?"

"It's about that human girl. Elizabeth. You bring hundreds of humans onto this planet, and then she's not special anymore, and she's safe. You're doing it for her."

I didn't say anything.

"Not going to deny it?"

"Of course I'm denying it," I said. "That would be a horrible thing for me to do, to cut off an entire planet from the rest of the galaxy for the sake of one girl."

"My point exactly," he said.

I looked up at him. "It's not for her."

"So, then you wouldn't care if I wanted her?"

I squared my shoulders, blinking at him.

He laughed. "You see?"

"You want her?"

"No, I'm making a point, Darce."

"You don't want her, then?"

"I don't *know* her," said Rehke. "Her hair is sort of intriguing, isn't it, though? It seems to be a number of different colors, and they aren't all visible except in the light, and then she's multifaceted and glowing and rather breathtaking."

I stared at him, unable to speak.

He stared back.

Finally, I wrenched my gaze back to the holoprojection. "The ship docks at the space station soon. After half a gemoon, this convoy departs, leaving the station with half the number of men to deal with, and I think that's the optimal time to strike."

"I agree," he said.

"I was going to ask you to come along with me when I take Elizabeth out to the Mooncross Ball. I didn't want to be passing her off to dance with men she didn't know, but I also didn't want it to look as if she were obliged to only dance with me."

"And now you're regretting it because you see me as competition."

I hesitated. "No." I took a deep breath. "It's not like that." *She doesn't like me, after all, and I haven't done much to recommend myself to her.*

"You *are* lying to yourself."

"It's best, honestly, if we keep the human girls away from the nobility as much as possible. Because the lower classes don't need a nobleman to organize a militia, and they definitely don't need the nobility in order to riot. We bring a hundred women and we give them to the lower classes, however?"

"You're not going to give the women to the

nobility?"

"How many children in your family, Rehke? Three, yes? Two in mine. How many children in a typical family of one of the greenhouse farmers?"

He sighed. "Well, that's disgusting. I thought you opposed the artificial insemination because you didn't want them treated like—"

"They will not be forced—"

"How is that any better than what our aunt was doing?"

"They'll have a *choice*," I snapped. "They'll be *courted*. They can all have multiple suitors, and even if men don't get mates, hopefully they'll get to share furs. At least there will be the hope of that."

"You know, maybe it would be better if you'd stop lying to yourself about how this is for the good of the planet," he said. "Maybe then, you'd just please yourself and work that little obsession out, and your mind would be clear to make better decisions in general."

"This is not about Elizabeth Bennet," I growled. "I kept the other one from Blenge, after all. Lied through my teeth to him and told him she was frightened of him. Once there are a number of women on the planet—"

"You'll need even more organization and more ability to protect them, and you'll need human women to consult with you." He lifted a finger. "You should just marry one of them and make her your co-heir to the seat."

"A human woman on the high seat? Are you as mad as the Toth?"

"Well, if we're taking this ship, we'll all be half-human within a generation, won't we?"

I blinked, thinking of that. "No, I'm not... I can't... I swear to you, I'm not doing this because I want that woman under my furs."

He chuckled.

"I'm serious," I said. "So serious that I don't care if you *do* want her. Do as you like."

He raised his brows, surprised.

"You'll be at the ball. You'll dance with her."

"I'll call upon her *daily*," he said.

I let out a long, slow breath. "Fine."

He laughed again. "Fine," he repeated, grinning at me in a way I didn't like.

TWELVE

Her Splendor sat at the head of the long table and looked me over in much the same way that Darce always did. Disapproval, bordering on disgust. We were here with her for dinner, and she was the only one speaking, and she was only speaking to me. Even Colle was uncharacteristically silent. It was only the four of us here: me, Charlotte, Colle, and Her Splendor Catte herself.

"At least you're not old," she said. "How old are you?"

I squared my shoulders and glanced at Charlotte, who was staring at her plate pointedly, as if to make it clear she'd have no part of this conversation. "Er, Your Splendor, on Earth asking a woman her age so bluntly, it's..."

"You can't be more than sixty mooncrosses," she said. "You have no reason to hide it."

Sixty? Well, there were three mooncrosses per Plembe-year, which were roughly equivalent to Earth-years, so she was actually remarkably spot on. I gave her a little smile. "Yes, about that, I guess."

"Hmm." She looked me over. "And you seem healthy enough, although you are frightfully pale. Your friend there, Charlotte, she's that same odd pinkish color but she looks much more robust. Furthermore, those spots all over you."

"Yes, my freckles," I said.

"But it's not as if you can do anything else," said Her Splendor.

"Anything else besides what?" I said.

"You have no skills that a woman would be prized for on Plembe. You can't read our language."

"I'd like to learn," I said. "But there hasn't been any real chance for that, and if I could be provided with a bracelet like seemingly everyone else has, perhaps I could? I don't mean to sound demanding, of course." I bowed my head on the last part. I wasn't even sure how I was supposed to be talking to this woman. Nothing had been explained to me.

"You don't know our dances. You aren't well-versed in our poetry or plays or history. You have no knowledge of culture. To have you mingle amongst our upper crust, it's preposterous."

"Well," I said, drawing myself up, "I was studying at a university on my planet, and I was well-versed in our culture, so it's not as if I'm incapable of learning such things."

She scoffed at this.

Wait, was I arguing with this woman? What was the point of it? I sighed. "But, yes, you're right, of course, Your Splendor, how backward and ignorant we must appear to you here."

"The only thing you could possibly excel at here on this planet is birthing babies," she said.

"Oh?" I found myself laughing. "So, *this* is your point."

"Yes, and I can't see why Darce would wish to subvert that or why he would think you could be presented to me, formally, as if you were daughters of the nobility, as if you two could ever be part of our society." She huffed. "It's preposterous," she repeated.

"Yes," I said with an exaggerated nod. "What *could* he be thinking?"

"So, you agree with me?" Catte lifted one of her hands. "Perhaps there's something reasonable within you yet."

I bit down on the inside of my lips to keep from snickering.

After the dinner, we all retired to a sitting room where a stringed instrument was set out. It was called a prah, and it was sort of like a harp, only all the strings were stretched out horizontally, as if over a table. Catte asked me if I had any experience playing one.

I obviously had not, but this didn't stop her from having me sit down at the thing and attempt to strum the thing and correct everything I did, even though I'd never *touched* one before.

Maybe this should have made me angry, but as the evening wore on, I began to find Catte more and more ridiculous. She was the preposterous one. She seemed entirely out of touch with anything that might allow her to properly rule a planet.

I needed to understand if there was some kind of representational government in place here or if it was a full-on monarchy. I had questions.

Luckily, I got to ask them the following day when Rehke and Darce appeared at Colle's house and we all went out to walk in the heated gardens in the center of town.

The gardens were encased in a large dome-like greenhouse sort of building. Inside, it was very warm, and there were paths through the most beautiful and colorful sorts of flowers, which had apparently been brought from all over the galaxy to grow here in this artificial habitat.

I had to admit that it was lovely, and I was awed by the beauty.

Rehke was pleasant and smiling, answering all my questions easily enough. Yes, there was an elected part of the government and it was balanced by another part of the government that was made up of nobles. Sort of like the House of Commons and House of Lords in England, I understood. Catte's position was not all-powerful, but she did have some authority.

Also, the entire galaxy had a set of rules and practices that all planets had to abide by and it set a certain standard of living. Slavery was never allowed; a certain standard of living for all members of the galaxy was required to be maintained and subsidized by the planetary government if necessary; all citizens must be given access to free treatment for life-threatening diseases. Failure to meet these things meant being cut off from the galactic senate, which also meant being cut off from the funding and protection such a thing conferred on the people of the galaxy.

It sounded like a workable system to me.

During all this, Darce was silent and solemn. He kept staring at me, and it was disconcerting that every time I looked up, I'd find his eyes on me.

Rehke was not as handsome as Darce. His features were a little less symmetrical, mouth twisting somewhat when he spoke, one eyebrow a bit cock-eyed. And yet, due to his easy manner and welcoming tone, I began to prefer looking at him than to look at Darce's scowl.

Darce only spoke up to tell me that the galactic

senate was being corrupted by the Toth. "Mark my words, it's a coup."

Rehke said, "He wants that to be true, of course, because then everything he's doing is justified."

Darce didn't say anything. He just glowered at Rehke.

Rehke lowered his voice conspiratorially. "I was going to come to see you on my own, and he wouldn't let me be alone with you. I can't see why. I'm perfectly trustworthy. Also, I know all about the flowers. This one, for example, is a red onia, from the planet Jarides."

"What's actually going on?" I said. "I'm part of some plan, but no one has thought to explain it to me."

"Ah, well, that's simple," said Rehke. "He wants to parade you around the capital city, showing everyone how civilized and sweet and winsome you are, and they'll be up in arms at that breeding idea our aunt had."

"Oh," I said. Maybe that plan was sort of obvious. I'd been over-complicating it in my brain.

"Yes, when do you want her to talk to the newsfeed media, Darce? At the Mooncross Ball?"

"There's a ball?" I said.

Rehke grinned at me. "You must be quite pitiful and talk about how terrified you were of the clinical nature of artificial insemination, because, of course, if you were going to have children, you'd rather do it the old-fashioned way. That will most certainly get the men of the planet on your side."

"No, don't say anything of the kind!" Darce was horrified.

"Oh, don't you want the men to imagine themselves having some sort of chance with her?" Rehke grinned widely at Darce.

"Definitely not," said Darce.

Rehke laughed.

"Thank you," I said quietly to Darce.

Rehke turned to me, tilting his head to one side. "Pardon me, that was insensitive of me, wasn't it?" He lifted one of his hands and turned it over. "What *do* we look like to you? Are you, in fact, terrified of us?"

I was flustered. "No, of course not. No, of course, you are all… quite… appealing." I looked away, drawing in a breath. "Of course, it's not completely unpleasant to have a number of men so, er, interested." I took a deep breath and changed the subject. "What kind of flower is that one?" I pointed.

"That's a blanet," said Rehke, barely looking at it. "So, then, why did you wish for the men not to feel as if they had a chance with you? Is it because you want the attentions of a specific one of us, one of us named Darce?"

I let out a wild laugh. "Don't be ridiculous."

Rehke was shocked by this and then he laughed too. He looked at Darce, delighted, laughed harder, and then turned back to me. "I see."

"Everyone seems to be convinced that Darce has some sort of designs on me, but he *told* me he thinks human women are disgusting," I said. "That's why I laughed. It's just ridiculous. And I don't… he and I…" I felt flustered.

"No, I do see," said Rehke.

"I don't know that you do," I said. "Of course I'm not terrified of any of you individually, but the idea of a large number of you, of many men all wanting to… share their furs with me or to f-force—

"No, no, of course." Rehke stopped me. "It seems I've been insensitive indeed."

Then, we were all quiet.

Belatedly, I said, "You weren't insensitive. I'm just—"

"You've been through quite a lot, Elizabeth," said Rehke. "I seem to have forgotten that for a moment while I was focusing on other things. What *do* you want? Perhaps you don't want to mate with one of our men at *all*."

I blushed. "W-well, I guess I—"

"That's insensitive as well," said Rehke, with a self-deprecating laugh. "You don't have to answer that very invasive, very personal question."

"It's all right." I looked up at him, and he was looking at me, and my breath caught in my throat. My voice was quiet. "Even on Earth, I guess I always wanted a family. I never knew my own parents, you see, so I guess I dreamed about being a mother and having my own children and having a husband that I loved to share that with. I do want..." I swallowed. "That."

"Yes," whispered Rehke, his gaze holding mine like a caress.

"We're blocking the path." Darce's voice was tight.

I looked down at my feet.

Darce pointedly began walking.

I went after him and Rehke brought up the rear.

Darce glanced at me. "You never told me that about your parents."

"Oh, are you interested in hearing personal tidbits about me, Darce?" I said. "Odd, because you never asked."

He flinched.

Rehke caught up to Darce and put a hand on his shoulder. "My cousin is often caught up in his own head. I can't tell you the number of times I've had entire conversations with him and he's not even paid a bit of attention."

Darce shrugged him off. "That's not true."

Rehke laughed. "It *is* true," he told me.

Darce sighed, looking annoyed. I couldn't understand why he was here at all. He seemed to be having a terrible time.

"Darce, you see, has no time for tidbits or anything else," said Rehke. "He must concern himself entirely with his duty. And between the two of us, he is the serious and grim one, whereas I, you see, am the fun one."

I laughed.

Darce shot his cousin a venomous look.

"Well, he *is* serious and grim," I said. "I can't deny that." I glanced at Rehke. "But I can't say I've seen proof of your claim to being the fun one."

"Ouch," said Rehke, grinning. "Well, I suppose that's a challenge, then, and when I rise to it, you'll have to eat your words."

I couldn't help but smile back.

"The question is, Elizabeth," he said, voice lowering, "what is it that you find fun?"

"Wouldn't you like to know?" I said. Oh, my. I was flirting with an alien, wasn't I? I kind of liked it. I could get used to it.

"Well, trial and error it is," he said. "Next time, I imagine Darce will stay home and leave us to it." He playfully drove his elbow into his cousin, who gave him a peevish look.

But the next day, when Rehke came back to see me, Darce came as well.

And this began a pattern that lasted a number of

pleiccs.

They would both show up, sometimes to take me somewhere public, making sure that the newsfeed media captured images of me looking at flowers or gliding on the frozen lake on a special pair of shoes that allowed me to cling to the ice. It wasn't quite like ice skates, but it was a similar feeling. We went to watch some sporting event that I couldn't follow. It was part race, part getting some small stone-thing into a net, and it spanned over a huge ice field.

But other times, we didn't go anywhere. We sat together in Colle's house, and sometimes he was with us, but other times, it was only Charlotte.

During all these times, Rehke was the only one who spoke. Darce was always there, always silent, always staring at me, and usually in a terrible mood the entire time. When he wasn't gaping at me, he was glaring at Rehke or telling his cousin to be quiet.

I learned all about Rehke.

His father and Darce's mother had been siblings. Since the line of succession on the planet went through women, Darce was ahead of him in line to the high seat. Rehke had never thought he'd ever be in line for it at all, but now, with their parents gone, and all the girls gone, including Rehke's sisters, there they were.

My heart went out to them, hearing this, because somehow I hadn't quite understood it, I didn't think. I hadn't realized that there had been so much death. They'd lost their mothers and sisters and then their fathers too. Their fathers had been caught up in the loss—heartbroken—and it had affected them. Darce's father had been in an accident in a tirecraft, but he'd been driving and Rehke said he hadn't been himself. Rehke's father, had gotten some other unrelated sickness, but he had seemed to have no will to keep going.

"I was all he had left," said Rehke. "His wife gone, both his daughters. He was too tired and broken to fight."

This had made me cry, and I'd wiped at my tears, while Rehke had admonished me, switching to telling jokes, apologizing for speaking of anything sad.

"You'll never think of me as the fun one now," he said with a smile, but his eyes were shining too.

During this time, the newsfeed media were reporting on my every move, and all of our outings were in direct response to anything Her Splendor said.

Her interviews on the subject were essentially replays of what she'd said at dinner. Human girls were healthy and pretty but useless for anything except baby making, and she couldn't see why we'd even *want* to do anything else.

So, then we went to art museums and a narle, which was a lot like an opera even though the singing style was different, all to show just how cultured I could be.

I was still not allowed to know where Jane and Lydia were, because this was an important secret, supposedly for their safety, but I was able to exchange messages with them.

Well. With Jane.

Lydia couldn't be bothered.

But apparently, they were in a very nice house, even bigger than Blenge's, and they were quite comfortable and enjoying all the amenities there, including a pool that Jane said was always filled with warm green water. A dip in it would ease all the soreness in your muscles, she said. She thought it was positively divine.

And pleiccs and pleiccs passed. The Mooncross Ball

was looming. I had to learn dances so that I could dance at this event, and I found the steps complicated and confusing. I practiced at home, mostly with Charlotte and Colle, because once I did practice with Darce, and all he did was criticize everything I did — from my posture to the way I moved on the wrong beat of the music. The more advice he gave me, the worse I got, so I banned him from my dance practices.

I was supposed to address the newsfeed media at this event, apparently, but Darce said that I should only talk about how much I wanted freedom to choose my own path, not anything at all about mating or breeding.

One evening, after dinner, Rehke did come alone.

We sat in the back of the holoroom, while Charlotte and Colle played a game that involved holographic rackets (like for tennis) and bopped various projectiles into a board for varying amounts of points.

"No Darce this time, I see," I said.

"I'm leaving soon," he said. "I, um, I don't know why Darce doesn't want you to know this, but I think you should know. I'm going along to oversee a military maneuver."

"Right, because you're in the military," I said. I kept forgetting this about him.

"We're capturing a ship full of hundreds of human women and bringing them here," said Rehke.

I sat up, blinking at him, lips parted, too stunned to know what to say.

"It'll be safer for you all once there are more of you," said Rehke.

Would it? I thought about it. I guessed it would be safer. But it was such an odd thing. "This is Darce's idea? But he hates human women."

"No, he doesn't." Rehke laughed this off. "It's odd

that you really can't see it, I suppose."

"See what?"

"Nothing." He chuckled to himself. "This is all for him, of course. I'm at his disposal."

"I imagine that's how he likes it," I muttered. "That's the way he is, after all."

"He's not a bad man, Elizabeth," said Rehke. "You don't seem to like him, but I wonder… it is only that I am just as he is, in the end, I suppose."

"You're nothing like him!" I protested.

"I mean, he is ruled by his duty, and so am I. And he and I were both raised to privilege, and I suppose we both are affected by that, perhaps sometimes badly. But I guess I…" He looked away, then, letting out another laugh.

I eyed him. He seemed almost nervous. "Is there something you're trying to say to me, Rehke?"

"I wouldn't dare ask to be your suitor, you know. I know Darce would—"

"I can have you as a suitor if I wanted," I said. "I accepted Wihke, after all, but I haven't seen him in a very long time."

"Wihke," said Rehke in a different voice. "How do you know Wihke?"

"He was one of the guards who was with us, until Darce came along and forced him to leave."

Rehke blinked. He got to his feet. "What did Darce tell you about Wihke?"

"What do you mean? Darce and I have never discussed him, not that—"

"And you and Wihke…" Rehke's lip curled. "What did you let him do?" Another chuckle, this one rueful. "Perhaps 'let' is the wrong word. No wonder you said that thing—"

"What are you talking about?" I said.

"Nothing," said Rehke, squaring his shoulders. "You should forget I said it, in fact, the thing about suitors and—"

"Because of Wihke?" I said. "You know, it was explained to me that women are allowed to have more than one, so I don't see why you're acting as though he's tainted me."

"No." He shook his head, surprised at that. "No, no, what a notion. Tainted?" He repeated that word. "Is that a thing that can happen to a woman?"

"Maybe not on your planet," I said.

He opened his mouth as if he was going to say something.

But I was already talking. "Is it just jealousy, then? Because Fannee did say—"

"Jealous of Wihke." Rehke scoffed as if that was impossible.

"So, then why?"

"He's serious," said Rehke.

"*Who* is serious about *what?*"

"About wanting to keep you away from the nobility," he said. "If he wasn't, he would have told you about Wihke. I suppose I should have known, after all, he did say that he lied to Blenge about the other one. What is her name? Jinn?"

"Jane?" I said. "Wait, what was all that? Tell me *what* about Wihke? And *how* did Darce lie?"

"Darce told Blenge that Jane was frightened of him," said Rehke.

"Why?"

"To keep him away from her. Blenge is not exactly nobility, but he's rich. He could buy and sell us all. No, it's best to keep the human women out of the upper classes, especially since there won't be enough of you to go around—"

"But Jane didn't want Darce to do that!" I exclaimed. "How dare he?"

"Oh, this isn't…" Rehke put up both hands. "I didn't mean to upset you."

"Of course I'm upset," I said. "I can't abide that man. I hate him. Darce is the most horrid being to crawl this planet." I clenched both of my hands into fists.

Rehke winced. "That's perhaps stating it a bit strongly, don't you think?" He let out a little laugh. "All right, look, I don't know. If I come back, if you're still interested, maybe—"

"*If* you come back?" Then it dawned on me. "This military mission, you could die."

"I won't." He grinned at me, an easy, unaffected grin.

"But you could?"

"No," he said. "Impossible."

"Why is Darce doing that?" I said. "Why is he bringing all those human women here?"

"To rescue them from the Toth?"

"But I thought if the Toth knew about even your rescuing us four, they'd retaliate."

"Yes, there are going to be consequences. But we're safe enough here. Our planet is surrounded by a lectre field. Nothing can penetrate it if we don't let it through. Don't worry. You'll be safe."

"Why would he do that?"

"I told you. It'll make you safer."

"But he doesn't care about—"

"Sure of that, are you?"

I drew back, speechless.

He closed the distance between us. He lifted a hand

and let it hover, close to my face, but he didn't touch me. His voice was soft now. "Elizabeth, I don't know if you have any idea how enchanting you are."

"Did Darce give the orders for you to go and risk your life? Is he the one putting you in danger?"

Rehke closed his hand into a fist and lowered his it. "I'll be fine." He squared his shoulders and looked at the door. "I should go. When I get back, I'll explain all of it. But I don't know if it's fair to make advances towards you when you don't know everything."

"What?"

"You might feel differently about him," Rehke said to his shoes.

"About who?"

"Men like me don't marry where they choose," he said, giving me another look, something longing, something that made my stomach flip over, and then he was gone, before I could even respond.

THIRTEEN

The dress Elizabeth wore to the Mooncross Ball looked as if it had been made of starlight. It was white, I supposed, but the fabric it had been made of shimmered and glittered, and it clung to her body in intriguing and mesmerizing ways. Her hair hung free around her shoulders like a glimmering cloud that was burnished orange and gold in the lights, and she was like some kind of raw force of nature come to life, like nothing I'd ever seen before.

Maybe that's why I did it.

I didn't plan it.

I just found myself ushering her off in the midst of it all, taking her to a small room off the main room where the dancing was taking place and shutting the door behind us, standing there in the doorway as if to bar her escape, as if somehow I knew she'd want to escape.

It was foolish to say what I said then. I knew nothing good would come of it. "You don't know what you do to me," I said to her. "You don't know how you torment me."

"Torment? I have not even spoken to you since we arrived this evening, and you have been staring at me like I'm some kind of roadkill—the way you always do—and I don't think—"

"What's roadkill?"

"Never mind." She sighed heavily. "Is this about what I'm going to say to the newsfeed media? Because I guess I wouldn't mind practicing that."

"You have to listen to me," I said. "You have to let me tell you how much I admire you. How much I am enamored by you. How I have somehow fallen in love with you no matter how I try not to."

She let out a noise in the back of her throat and backed up, backed all the way into the far wall.

"I know this is a surprise to you, because I've done my best to conceal it. I hoped you might have suspected, however, since I been spending so much time with you lately. I thought you might have seen how much it pained me when Rehke flirted with you."

She only shook her head.

"I admit it's not an ideal match," I said. "I am meant to marry someone of my species, someone of the nobility. I also have the idea that I'd rather not have members of the nobility taking the human girls, and if I were to marry you, then how could I deny them? It won't set a proper precedent. It's really going to be disastrous, truly, the entire idea of it. Which is why I have not allowed myself to even entertain it. I have struggled and fought internally to end this entire notion of ever being with you. I can't ask to be your suitor. I can't marry you. And yet, here I am, begging for that exact thing. Accept me as a suitor, Elizabeth. I can't live without you."

She let out another noise.

I waited.

"You…" She squared her shoulders. "What is wrong with you?"

I furrowed my brow. "Wrong with me?"

"Is it customary on your planet to tell a girl that you like her a lot, but only against your better judgment?"

"Well, no, but it's simply the truth. I wasn't going to lie to you."

"Oh, no, you don't *lie*, I suppose."

"I try not to."

"Except to Blenge."

I let out a breath. "I did, yes. To him I have been kinder than I have been to myself." I tilted my head. "Who told you of that? Was it Rehke?"

"Rehke, the one you've sent on a dangerous mission to capture more human women for no reason I can possibly fathom? Except now I wonder if you were trying to get rid of him so that you wouldn't have any competition for me."

"Compet..." I drew myself up. "Has he asked to be your suitor?"

"Maybe he has." Her eyes flashed.

I looked away. "Oh."

"And that's leaving out whatever it was you did to Wihke."

"What *I* did to Wihke?"

"He said you deprived him of his inheritance that your father left to him."

"He said that? Ah, well, that sounds like something he'd say." I felt rage rising in me at Wihke's name, rage and pain and horror and confusion.

"And also, Darce, when I met you, you said you could barely tolerate looking at me—"

"That is not exactly what I—"

"Then you said that I looked diseased and that human women were disgusting. Then you tried to force me into some kind of breeding program—"

"Well, I changed my mind about that."

"But from the beginning, I have known you are the last man in the entire universe I could ever accept as a suitor!"

That hurt. I swallowed, looking away.

"Oh, I didn't mean it to sound…" Her voice died out.

"Yes, you did," I said. "Obviously, this is your opinion of me. Why I'm surprised, I'm not sure." I squared my shoulders. "Very well, let's talk about speaking to the newsfeed media."

"What? There's no way I can do that right now. I'm way too flustered." She came for me.

At first I didn't know what she was doing. It was almost as if she was coming to kiss me, except for that look on her face, that angry look, her gold-flecked eyes flashing at me.

Then she reached around and palmed the controls for the door.

I moved out of the way.

She swept past me.

I hung my head and tried to collect myself. What had I been thinking?

Idiot, Darce, you're an idiot.

When I raised my gaze, she was across the room, standing with Rehke, and I could see that she was speaking animatedly, gesturing with her hands.

Well, you brought that on yourself, I told myself. I had, after all, told him I didn't care if he wanted her. I'd given him my blessing. It wasn't as if he didn't realize, however, how I felt about her.

Foolishly, I'd thought he was flirting with her only to taunt me, that he was trying to make some point, and that it wasn't about her, only about…

But of course he wanted her.

Who wouldn't?

I was having trouble breathing. Now, it was going to destroy me, however, the two of them together. It might have been one thing if I'd never said anything to her, but having given it words, having said them aloud, it somehow made my feelings more powerful. I had wanted her a long time, since practically the first moment I clapped eyes on her, truly, and now it was all impossible.

She hates me. I shied away from the thought, but I knew it was true, and I understood why as well. It only made sense for her to hate me. In some ways, it was even deserved. I had done abominable things, said things that were even worse, and she had no reason to think well of me. None at all.

But if Rehke was what she wanted and if he wanted her too, I'd have to find some way to make my peace with it. It wouldn't be easy, of course, and I didn't know how I'd manage it, seeing them together, watching her bear his children, spending my whole life with her connected to my closest family member. It sounded like torture, but I could do it.

Rehke deserved happiness. He'd been through so much.

I needed to take him off the mission. He was supposed to leave this evening, midway through the ball, but I couldn't let him go, not now. If Elizabeth lost him, it would hurt her, and I couldn't risk that, couldn't risk him. Truthfully, I wouldn't have risked him as it was. I didn't want to. But I couldn't keep my family members safe, not when I was asking the people of my planet to undertake dangerous missions on my orders. If my people had to make sacrifices, so did I. I had to accept those consequences. It was what a ruler did.

Now, though, for Elizabeth… if it was for her, I'd do anything.

Rehke was right.

I was doing all this for her. I was being reckless and taking risks—with other people's lives—for that woman. It was madness.

I was never going to stop, though, not even if she was my cousin's wife.

I was devoted to her. I didn't know why. It was wrong. It was dangerous, even. But it was irrevocable.

FOURTEEN

elizabeth

"You're here." I looked him over, shaking my head.

Rehke nodded. "So I am."

"You said you were going on a military mission!" This sounded more like an accusation that I really meant it to, but I was in a emotional state right now. I was also in a very sparkly dress. The sparkles and the anger and the confusion and… and Darce? It was all *impossible.*

"I am," he said.

How could Darce say that? How could he be in love with me? "You made it sound like you were saying goodbye," I said.

"Well, I'm leaving in…" He checked his bracelet. "Three hihors, so it'll be in the middle of the ball. I didn't know if we'd really get much chance to talk, and this didn't seem like the place to talk about… but then I didn't even ask you…" He sighed. His gaze flicked over me, and then his voice changed. "You look amazing."

I bit down on my lower lip. "You're going to tell me about Wihke now."

"No," he said. "No, not here."

"Yes, here," I said. "You can tell me while we dance." I thought about that. Well, maybe not, because

I still had to concentrate a lot to remember all of the dance steps. I looked up to see that the room that I'd been in with Darce was empty and Darce wasn't there anymore.

I seized Rehke's hand and tugged on him. "All right, not while we dance. We'll go there, where I was just speaking with Darce."

"But aren't you supposed to speak to the newsfeed media?" he said.

"Come with me," I said, tugging hard on his hand.

He let me pull him with me and we started across the dance floor.

Halfway there, we were intercepted by several men, who were holding up their wrists with their bracelets, ready to record me. "Elizabeth, there you are. Can we do our interview now?"

"Can it wait?" I said.

"Just a few questions," said one of them.

"It won't take long," said the other.

"I just... I don't want to be bred," I said. "And anyway, apparently, there are going to be hundreds of human women here soon, so—"

"*Elizabeth!*" Rehke yanked on my hand. To the men, "She's not talking to the newsfeed media right now."

"What?" I said, looking up at him. "Is that supposed to be a secret?"

"Yes, of course!"

"Well, you didn't *say* that," I said.

He was pulling me away from the men with their bracelets, who had excited wide-eyed looks, because I guessed I'd just given them the scoop of the mooncross. Oops. "I can't believe you thought you should tell that to the newsfeed media."

"I didn't know I shouldn't," I protested.

And then we were finally in that room, and the door was whisking closed, shutting us inside alone together.

He went over to the wall and rested his forehead against it, shutting his eyes. "Ice gods of the blanic horizon."

"I'm sorry," I said. I was. "They were going to find out eventually."

"If my aunt finds out, she could stop it." He turned on me. "I have to go. We need to get off the ground before—"

"Tell me about Wihke."

"Oh, for the sake of all the gods and all the ice, Elizabeth." He clenched both of his hands into fists.

I stood in the doorway. "There's something to tell, and you said I might feel differently about Darce if I knew it, and—"

"Why do you care about—" His eyes widened. "Darce asked to be your suitor."

"Well, I told him no."

"But you want me to change your mind?"

"I…" No. That wasn't what I wanted. Only… why was I coming to him for this information?

He sighed heavily. "Of course you do. Of *course* you do."

"I hate him," I said. "And you are… you're everything he's not. You're funny and easy to talk to and… and fun. You *are* the fun one. I think if you did ask me to be your suitor, I'd be an idiot to say no."

"But *would* you say no?"

"I just said that I wouldn't."

"That's not what you said." He rubbed his forehead. "It's fine. I couldn't be with you anyway."

"I would say yes to you over him a thousand times," I said firmly.

He let out a bitter laugh. "He and I, we're all each other has, you realize that? He's lost everyone and so have I. We're cousins, but we're more like brothers. He loves you, and I could never do that to him, in any case. It would break my bond with him, and I love him, and—" He shook himself. "This doesn't matter. I need to go."

"Rehke, I—"

"Darce had a sister," said Rehke. "Her name was Gige. She was younger than him, but she was third in line to the high seat, after Catte's daughter and Darce's mother. She was only forty-five mooncrosses old."

I did the math on that. Fifteen Earth-years. Just a girl.

"She had an inheritance. It's not uncommon for women in the nobility to bring money into a marriage. It's one of the reasons they might have so many suitors competing for them? But she was too young for suitors. She hadn't even been presented to Her Splendor. And no one was doing that anyway, because of the disease. All the women were in quarantine, and they were being kept from everyone."

"Right, there would have been a quarantine," I whispered.

"She was young. She didn't like being cooped up. And Wihke..."

"Wihke?" I said.

"You've met him. You know what he's like. He convinced her to leave the quarantine. He took her with him and he, erm, well, he 'convinced' her to share his furs, but when she told us of it, it sounded like coercion to me, and we got there before he could 'convince' her to marry him, which was what it was all about, of course, her inheritance. Well, maybe it was just about sex. I don't know. What was he like with you?"

I was shaking. I didn't say anything. I was thinking about the way he'd moved my hand onto his erection, the way he'd made me stroke him, the way I'd thought, *I guess we're doing this.*

"We stopped the marriage," said Rehke. "Darce and I both. His mother was already dead. My mother was sick. Our fathers were useless at that point, and we were both... we protected the wealth, though, oh, yes." He was bitingly sarcastic. "Darce and I were quite good at doing that. As for Gige..."

"She died," I breathed. "She got sick because he took her out to seduce her, and then she died."

It was quiet. The look on his face let me know that I'd gotten it right.

"I have to go, Elizabeth," he said, palming the door open.

I was speechless. I was trying to sort out everything that I'd felt about Wihke, including that awful night when he'd broken into my room and I'd begged him to save me. He'd promised he was coming back, but he hadn't come back, and he'd been very obsessed with... with... Was he just the sort of man who would say anything to get me to give him a hand job? Was *that* who he was? Because the evidence, it was leaning towards that, and the worst thing was that I had felt frightened of him and I'd talked myself out of it. He'd somehow gotten into my head and made my own brain work against me in his favor.

Oh, and his sob story about how Darce had treated him badly?

I rushed out of the room after Rehke, holding the skirts of my dress. I fell into step with him. "Wait, the inheritance, is that a lie?"

"What are you talking about?" said Rehke.

"Wihke says that Darce denied him credits that Darce's father left for him."

Rehke was still walking. "I really don't have time to talk to you right now, Elizabeth. I need to get those ships off the ground if we're going to make this attack on the space station."

"Is it a lie?"

"Yes."

"So, there was no inheritance?"

"Darce's father left Wihke land," said Rehke, looking across the room as he walked even faster, barely paying attention to me. "It had a greenhouse on it, and it was the sort of thing where if Wihke had taken control of it, he could have sold the food that was grown there and it would have been a business, and he could have supported himself, even a family. It was an amazing gift. But he wanted it liquid, and he asked Darce for the value of it instead, and they haggled over how much it was worth, and Darce gave him an amount that I thought was more than fair, but..."

"Wihke spent it all," I said.

"And came back for more." Rehke turned to me. "Elizabeth, really, I can't—"

"Rehke, can I speak to you?" It was Darce. Where had he come from? He glanced at me. "In private?"

"I don't have time," said Rehke. "You might not realize this, but Elizabeth here just told the newsfeed media that hundreds of human women are coming to the planet."

Darce turned on me.

I cringed. "I'm sorry. But you got me all out of sorts with confessing your feelings—"

"Anyway, I need to go," said Rehke. "If we don't get those ships in the air right away, our aunt could order them all to stand down. This mission only works if she's ignorant of it. She wouldn't approve."

"All right, yes," said Darce. "But you're not going."

"What? I have to go," said Rehke.

"If something happens to you..." Darce looked at me. "Can we speak away from her?"

"I'm not speaking at all." Rehke burst past his cousin and me and hurried toward the door.

Darce pursued him.

I picked up my skirts and went too.

"I won't force her to lose you," Darce was saying. "If the two of you—"

"She wants *you*," said Rehke, rounding on Darce.

"I assure you, she does *not*," Darce growled.

And then they both turned and looked at me.

I froze in place.

Rehke let out a noise of frustration. "I don't have *time* for this." And then he was moving again.

Darce looked at me, his jaw working. Finally, he said, in a mangled voice, "Elizabeth. I'm very sorry if I got you, er, out of sorts. I'm sorry for a number of..." He looked into Rehke's wake. "I'll keep him from going. I won't let anything happen..." He sighed. "If you'll excuse me." He hurried after Rehke.

I watched them both go, and I didn't go after them.

When I turned around, the men from the newsfeed media were there, recording me.

"Do you have any suitors, Elizabeth?" asked one.

I couldn't help it. I laughed. One long, harsh laugh that went on and on and made me sound crazy.

And then I fled.

FIFTEEN

"They really all do like you," said Charlotte, shaking her head at me. "*All* of them."

"No," I said. "Not all of them." I thought about it. "Forste never did. Or Denne. Or Blenge, for that matter. And I'm not convinced Colle ever really liked me either. I think he would have been happy with any of us."

"Well, thanks for that," said Charlotte.

We were in my bedchamber at Charlotte's house, both sitting on my bed. I'd forced her to take me home from the ball, which had meant that Colle had to leave too, and he hadn't been especially pleased about that, but Charlotte really was good at soothing him.

"Sorry, I didn't mean…" I sighed. "I really am sorry that you had to marry him to manipulate him, and —"

"He's not so bad," she said.

"Oh, well, that's saying something, then."

She laughed. "All right, when he talks, he…" She rolled her eyes.

"Yes," I said.

"But he loves me, Elizabeth. He worships me." She let out a little laugh, a different laugh, and I saw something come over her features that I didn't think I'd seen before. She reached out and took my hand. "I want you to listen to me, because I'm older than you."

"Charlotte, I don't think—"

"When I was your age, I didn't like myself very much," she said. "And I had this idea that anyone who *did* like me must be damaged and idiotic in some way, and therefore unworthy of me. Do you understand? If a boy treated me with disdain and wasn't very nice to me, I was immediately attracted to him, because he seemed aspirational, right? Maybe I could win his love, and then it would *mean* something."

I blinked at her. "Look, it's not like that with Darce."

She raised her eyebrows. "Oh, interesting."

"What's interesting?"

"Let me finish my point first," she said. "I missed out on all these guys who would have been good for me, because I wanted love to be an adventure."

"Well..." I sat up. "I see what you're saying, but shouldn't there be some kind of passion in a relationship?"

"No," she said. "I think passion is overrated. Passion equals pain. And let's be honest, what has Darce caused you thus far? Nothing but pain."

"Well... I mean, I don't like him."

She didn't say anything.

"I don't," I muttered. "Anyway, I think it's just all been a misunderstanding or something? He hasn't told me everything."

"You're making excuses for him." She shook her head at me. "You should obviously pick Rehke. So he's got a crooked face, who cares? He's the right choice."

I twisted my hands together in my lap. I shrugged. "I agree with you."

"It doesn't sound like you do, actually."

"Darce has a lot to answer for," I said. "What he did

to Blenge and Jane, for instance?"

"Exactly," she said.

"And he should have told me about Wihke," I said. "If I'd known what Wihke had done to Darce's sister, I would never have trusted him."

"Very good point."

"So," I said, standing up, "maybe I should find him and get him to explain those things to me."

She scoffed. "No, you should definitely not do that."

"I don't even know *how* I'd do that," I said. "Has it escaped your notice that none of us have bracelets?" I lifted my bare wrist, as if to illustrate the point.

"We can't read their language and everything on the networks is in that language, so Colle says it's pointless," said Charlotte.

"Well, maybe we could learn if we had them," I said. "That's another thing I'm going to say to him."

"To who? Colle?"

"No, to Darce." I went across the room to the door and palmed it. It opened up. I looked down at myself. I was still wearing my dress from the ball. "Do you think he's still at the Mooncross Ball?"

"Colle will lose his mind if we try to go back there," said Charlotte, coming after me.

But she was wrong.

I found Colle downstairs, and he was overjoyed at the prospect of going back to the ball, because he hadn't wanted to leave in the first place.

We all climbed back into the tirecraft and went across town to the ballroom. It was late, and the party had definitely thinned out. Also, Catte had discovered that the ships had taken off for the space station, but she wasn't actually angry about such a thing. Instead, she seemed to think it was a brilliant idea and latched onto Colle immediately, telling him how a breeding program could repopulate the entire planet if it had hundreds of women, and what a superb idea it was, and how she'd thought of it herself.

But I couldn't find Darce.

The newsfeed media guys came to ask me more questions. Instead, I asked them if they'd seen Darce.

They agreed to contact him on their bracelets if I would answer some questions for them, and they turned out to be silly sort of questions, in the vein of what my likes and dislikes were and what I looked for in a man, that kind of thing.

Darce appeared at the end of these questions and yanked me away from them, despite their protestations and I—for no reason I could really even fathom—fitted my hand into his, linking our fingers.

He looked down at our entangled digits and his expression went agonized.

My voice came out scoured. "You have things to explain. Lots of things. Because the only rational way I could possibly feel about you right now is to dislike you."

"Of course," he murmured.

"Can we go somewhere to talk about those things?" Why did I sound out of breath?

He did too, if it came to that. "Somewhere alone?"

"Somewhere very private," I said.

His fingers tightened on mine. "I couldn't stop him."

"Rehke, you mean? He went on the mission?"

"Yes," he whispered harshly. He was leading me now. We were walking. He took me to his tirecraft. "Shall I send a message to Colle that I'll see you home later?"

"Yes," I said. "Charlotte would worry otherwise."

We got into the tirecraft. Every other time I'd traveled with him, he'd sat on one side, and I'd sat on the other side, facing him. But this time, we sat next to each other on one seat, and he pulled a fur on the floor up over both of us, and I burrowed into his heat.

I had lots and lots of things to say to him.

However, I didn't say any of them.

He let go of my hand and put his arm around me, tucking my smaller body into his large one.

I shut my eyes and lay my head against his warm, firm chest.

I could hear his heart beating—very fast—and it was soothing and familiar, like he wasn't some other species. I pressed even closer.

"If Rehke dies..." Darce's voice was deep and booming and I could hear it resonating in his chest, because my ear was pressed into it.

"He said he wouldn't," I said.

"If he does, you'll hate me."

"I already hate you," I said.

He laughed helplessly. "Well, then."

I looked up at him, pressed in against his chest.

He reached down and cupped my cheek with one hand. "Elizabeth..."

I looked into his eyes and then down at his lips and then back to his eyes. It was invitation, and I saw he understood.

He made a guttural noise in the back of his throat and then he put his mouth on mine.

At first, the kiss was very careful. It was gentle and hesitant. But as I responded to him, the kiss seemed to pick up heat, like a fire kindling to life, until it grew heated and fierce, and we were so caught up in it we didn't notice that the tirecraft had stopped, not until someone from outside was saying Darce's name.

Then we jerked apart, no longer touching, and the fur we'd been under slithered down to the floor of the tirecraft.

Darce was shaking. He looked at me, his expression full of questions.

"Your Senn?" came the voice from outside again.

"Yes," he replied, hoarse, his voice shaking too. He lurched over me and opened the door to the tirecraft.

I drew in a breath and let it out.

He was climbing out.

I moved forward.

He helped me out of the craft.

That was when I realized he'd taken me to the palace. Which made sense, I guessed. He did live here.

He was speaking to the man who'd been outside the craft, someone who worked here, I thought, but in a low voice, and I couldn't make it out.

The man nodded and took off into the palace.

Darce and I followed him.

Inside, it was much warmer. We followed the man into a transroom and went up several levels and then over. The door opened into a room with several stuffed chairs in it. There was an open doorway, and through it, I saw there was a bed.

Oh. Were we in Darce's *bedroom?*

My heart skipped a beat.

Darce went over and shut the door to the room with the bed. He ran a hand through his hair, flustered.

The servant who'd brought us here was busying himself pulling things out of a cabinet, setting out a tablecloth on a small table. He went over and opened a door in the wall, and there was a tray of food—fruits that were grown in the greenhouses here and smoked meat and cheeses. He set them down on the table and looked up at Darce, who dismissed him.

Then the servant left, and it was me and Darce.

Alone.

In his bedroom.

He gestured. "I wasn't thinking. I don't know why I brought you…" He squared his shoulders. "There are other places we could have talked."

"Talked," I repeated.

"That's why we're here. You said that I had things to explain."

"You do." I nodded.

Then, it was completely silent for some time.

Finally, I said, "This thing with you, it doesn't make sense to me."

"What thing?"

"You *know* what thing."

"I obviously don't know or I wouldn't have asked."

"I want a bracelet," I said.

"You don't have…" He looked at my hand.

"I want to learn how to read your language, and to speak it too, really speak it, not with this." I touched the translator in my ear.

"Of course," he said. "That's… it's abominable you've been here this long and no one has thought to do anything about that." He lifted a finger. "One hisec." He turned and palmed the door to the room with the bed open. He disappeared inside and then he came back with a small round piece of metal. He flicked it open and it was a projection of words. English words.

I gasped.

"When, um, when I scanned the Toth ship to determine they had women, there were a number of files on Earth languages and customs, and I uploaded them all to… anyway, our software has scanned this and it's able to do translations. I don't know how well they're rendered, but… this is my favorite book. I had it translated so that you could read it. I know you said you liked to read, so I thought…"

I smiled. "This is…" Why did my heart feel like it was expanding? "Thank you."

"There were texts of a number of Earth books that I could have translated the other way," he said. "If you want to tell me some of your favorites and I can find them, perhaps we could trade books with each other, and then… er, talk about them, if that's something you'd—"

"Perfect," I said, grinning madly at him. "That sounds perfect." I set down the book he'd given me, and the holoprojection turned off when I did. I closed the distance between us and I put my hand on his chest.

"I thought I was meant to be… explaining…"

"You are," I said. I slid my hand up his chest, all the way up, and I hooked my hand around the back of his neck. I pulled his face down to mine. "Definitely explain."

He was kissing me again.

I groaned into his mouth.

He put his hands on my waist. He slid them down to my hips. His tongue was in my mouth. He pulled me close, pulled our bodies flush, and I was pressed into him, and he was solid and huge and warm.

But, with a guttural noise, he pulled away. "I'm quite confused right now," he said thickly.

I laughed. "Me too."

"What about Rehke?"

"I thought I could have you both as suitors. I thought that was allowed."

"So, you *are* accepting me as a suitor?" he said.

"Clearly."

"You said you hated me."

"I do," I said. "I mean... I don't know. I'm very confused, too."

He laughed.

I kissed him again. This kiss was slippery and full of heated promise, his tongue moving in my mouth—so different than Wihke's had, even though it was that same sort of agile tongue. Darce kissed *with* me, whereas Wihke had just taken over me.

And I didn't want to think about Wihke at all, I found.

Instead, I dragged my hand down over Darce's shoulder, feeling the firmness of his muscle beneath, and then I slid my palm down over his chest. I realized his shirt had an eazclasp, and I parted it, baring a hint of his blue chest to me. He was covered in a dusting of dark hair, and I touched that, making it stand up under my fingertips.

Darce made a strangled noise. "Elizabeth."

I looked up at him. Maybe I was going too fast, trying to push Wihke out of my head. Maybe I should slow down. "I'm sorry," I breathed.

"It's not..." He laughed. "I don't mind, not at... at all, it's only..."

"I know," I whispered. "But..." I licked my lips. "What if we did this first and then talked afterwards?"

He laughed again. "Well..."

I kissed him lightly on the lips, pulling his shirt farther open, baring more of his beautiful, blue, rippling chest. "I think it's a very good idea, personally."

"I don't really have any objections," he said in a guttural voice. "But I'm not sure it's an entirely intelligent way to go about things."

"Mmm," I said. "Maybe not."

"I don't seem to *be* intelligent when it comes to you, I admit." He winced. "Oh, dear, I didn't mean that the way it sounded."

"I know what you meant." I had a hand inside his shirt now, tracing the swells of his pectoral muscles, relishing the way I could feel his strength and how — uncovered — he seemed so vulnerable.

"If you hate me, Elizabeth…" His breath hitched as my hand moved on him. "Then it would be the height of villainy to take advantage of you in this way. I'm not… I wouldn't… We need to stop."

"Stopping would be the smart thing," I agreed in a soft voice. I had his shirt entirely open at this point. I peeled it away from his shoulders. Then I paused. "Wait, do you want me to stop? Am I making you uncomfortable or coercing you or — "

"I'm not uncomfortable," he said in a gravelly voice. "That's not exactly the sensation I'm having at the moment."

Good. I didn't want to be forceful like Wihke at all. Oh, *why* did I keep thinking about him? I reached back and found the eazclasp on my own dress and yanked. The bodice came open and it fell forward, exposing me — my breasts were bare underneath, because the dress had a built-in supporter.

A sharp intake of breath from Darce.

I looked up at him.

He was staring at my bare skin.

I couldn't help but smile at that. I arched my back,

pushing my breasts out.

"You…" His voice was ragged. "May I…" He lifted a hand.

"Please," I breathed.

One of his six-fingered huge blue hands cupped me gently. His palm covered me, and the tip of my breast puckered at the sensation, and I gasped.

He let out an answering noise and then rubbed a finger over the hardened nub.

I shut my eyes. That shot through me like a rocket.

And then his other hand was on my other breast, and he teased that tip too, and I moaned as he rubbed and plucked me, making the pleasure volley through me, soaring all the way to the center of me—which was becoming tight and molten.

He pulled me closer and I opened my eyes to see him bending down and then his tongue—his long, flexible tongue—started to taste the hardened tips of my breasts, and that was out of this *world*.

I clutched his shoulders for balance, and I started making noises, embarrassing noises that wrenched their way out of me and he just kept at it, making long, slow unhurried strokes with that tongue of his, thoroughly tasting and exploring me.

It went on and on, and by the time he was kissing my mouth again, one hand on one of my breasts, I was loose and warm and eager—even though the center of me was tight, coiled and ready to spring.

He was somehow completely without his shirt at that point, and my dress was hanging precariously on my hips. My bare belly was pressed into his pelvis, and I could feel that he was excited too, could feel him straining against his pants.

I put my hand on him there, cupped him through his

clothes, and he jerked against me, letting out a surprised grunt.

I liked that. I grinned up at him.

His expression had grown soft. I'd never seen him look quite like that. He traced one blue finger over the swell of my breast. "I got carried away. Were we talking about stopping?"

"That's not going to happen," I said. "We're too far gone."

"We're not," he said, but he was smiling.

I squeezed him through his pants again.

His eyes rolled back in his head. "It would be… easier to stop if you weren't doing… that."

I squeezed him again, grinning. "I don't want to stop."

"Well, I don't either, but it's not about what we want, it's about—"

"Yes, it is." I kissed him.

He sighed.

Our tongues tangled in a very, very nice way.

When I pulled back, I nodded over his shoulder. "Is that your bed?"

He smiled, looking sheepish. "I swear to you, I didn't plan for this to—"

"You want to show it to me?"

He laughed. "Are you sure?"

"Positive."

"Right, then."

I reached back and undid the eazclasp of my dress entirely, stepping out of it.

His eyes widened.

I was now wearing nothing except a pair of sinces, which were basically like very clingy long underwear. Everyone wore them because of the cold, and they did keep a person pretty warm, but the material was thin.

He was touching me, his hand over the sinces, gliding over my backside, down to my thigh, and then back up again, to the small of my back. He kissed my temple. "You're beautiful," he gasped into my skin. "You take my breath away."

I kissed him again.

He gathered me into his arms.

We kissed in a frenzy, until I pulled away, both my palms against his bare blue chest. "You know," I wheezed, "you're nice to look at yourself. You're also… I mean… your shoulders are…" I put my hands on them, the span of them.

He gazed at me, half-lidded eyes full of pleasure. "I like that I please you, because you're… everything about you…" His fingers splayed out over my collarbone. "Your freckles, the way they fade out, the way you're creamy all over your breasts, except for…" He touched one freckle next to my aureole.

I was blushing.

"That one," he said. "And then…" His fingers walked across to another freckle, on the underside of my breast. "There." Suddenly his mouth was on me there.

I gasped.

"I want," he breathed into my skin, "to kiss every single one of them."

I moaned. "I won't argue with that."

He swept me up, off my feet, and carried me into the other room.

And then we were on the bed, and we were kissing again, our bodies horizontal, everything lined up quite indecently, my sinces and his pants the only thing between the pulsing heat of our pelvises as we writhed against each other.

There was a beeping noise from outside the room, and he pushed up on his arms, making an annoyed face.

"What?" I whispered.

"My apologies, but I need to…" He climbed off the bed and left the room. When he came back, he had his bracelet, but he wasn't wearing it. He simply had it in one hand, and he was scrolling through a holoprojection of alien letters, brow furrowed.

I propped myself up on my elbows. "What is it? Is it Rehke?"

He pulled up something that looked like a holoprojection of a keyboard and typed furiously.

"Darce, is Rehke okay?"

He lowered the bracelet. "He's fine. I mixed up the order of a few numerals in the access codes. I've corrected it. It's fine." He sat down at the edge of the bed. "It's fine."

I swallowed. I felt a little self-conscious and flung an arm over my breasts, hunching my shoulders.

"It's fine," he repeated, setting his bracelet down on a table next to the bed. "I shouldn't be doing this with you. At all, probably, but definitely not right now."

"I know," I whispered. "It's my fault. You've been saying that all along."

He looked up at me. "You're covering yourself?"

"You just said…"

He crawled up the bed to me, gently pulling my arm away, revealing me to him again. He gazed at my bare skin in awe, his breath hitching.

"Darce…" I breathed.

"I know," he muttered. Suddenly, he was pulling on my sinces, peeling them off me, and I wasn't wearing anything under them at all, and my heart started to beat fast and wild, and I helped him. Together we divested me of the rest of every stitch I was wearing, and then my hands went to the clasp of his pants, which parted easily under my fingers. Without his clothes encasing him, he burst out into my palm, and he was blue and stiff and huge and kind of… pretty.

I ran my finger over the head of him, the tip, which was a sort of greenish blue color, like the sea before a storm, and he groaned.

I sighed.

He pushed me back into the bed and kissed me, kicking his pants off at the same time.

Now, we were both entirely bare, and his skin was warm and soft against mine. He settled between my thighs and I moved one of them, rubbing the inside of my leg against his hip.

He used his tongue on my breasts again, and then my belly and then he looked at me, and he grinned. "Oh, it *is* adorable."

"Adorable?" I said, confused.

"The patch of hair. Blenge said—" He cringed. "Oh, ice gods of the horizon, forget I—"

"You and Blenge were discussing—"

"No!" He shook his head. "Not in any real detail. I swear to you, I would never say anything about you—"

"It's actually okay," I said, thinking of the conversations all of us women'd had with each other about our forays into alien lovemaking. "I get it. What I don't get is, um, adorable."

He stroked my mound, grinning wickedly.

I sighed, arching my back, my breath getting stuck in my throat.

And then his fingers were other places, parting the

folds of me, brushing against my most sensitive of spots and then his *tongue* —

I cried out.

He lapped at me.

I wanted to writhe and stay still at the same time. I wanted to scream and I couldn't scream. I panted, but I was frozen, and his tongue molded itself over the nub of me there, licking the concentrated center of me, licking all around the center, licking me in the best of ways.

I shuddered and gasped and my legs started to shake.

He pulled away and tapped his finger against me there. "You're very sensitive here."

"Your women... have..."

"Yes," he said, laughing. "Mostly the same, but... maybe not quite so sensitive. The way you *taste*, though..." His voice was guttural.

He *liked* that?

Okay, I was keeping him. I was never letting him go, and he was perfect, and I wanted —

His tongue swept over me again and all thoughts were swept away with each tantalizing flick.

My hips jerked.

Not in any kind of rhythm, not with his movement, just out-of-control movements that I would have been embarrassed about except for the fact that it felt too good, and I was surrounded in the sweetest and most wonderful of sensations. His tongue picked me up like some kind of magic carpet and carried me all the way into the starry sky overhead, and I hovered there, floating over the icy horizon, each movement of his mouth taking me further and further and further into my pleasure...

And then he stopped.

At first, I was too surprised to even understand what had happened. I opened my eyes and I found him over me, his face inches from mine, smiling at me. He kissed me, and the taste on his tongue, it was sort of tart and musky, and maybe it wasn't unpleasant, maybe… I let him kiss me, but I pushed away. "Did you have to stop?" I whispered.

He smiled a wide, wide smile. "I want to feel you come around me," he murmured in a husky voice. "Can we do that?"

"I…" I touched his face, his perfect and massive shoulder. "I don't know if that'll work."

"No?" he said.

"I've never been able to, um, to do that *during*," I said in a tiny voice. Not that I had massive amounts of experience. In terms of orgasms with partners, I'd only ever had one with Biff once, and it had definitely not been during intercourse. He'd complained about how it had given his hand a cramp, about how long it had taken me.

"Well, if not, I'll finish you afterwards," he said in an easy, smooth, deep voice, as if that was nothing to him, as if getting me off was a foregone conclusion, and I'd never experienced that level of confidence from a man, but it was… well, he *was* arrogant, wasn't he?

I summoned some sort of imperiousness. "I will hold you to that."

His smile widened. "So… then… can I…? Will you take me, Elizabeth?"

I stroked his shoulder. "Of course. I wouldn't have let it get this far if I wasn't planning on… on…"

He kissed me again. His voice was a rasp, even as he reached between us and began to rub the tip of his hardness against my very wet—when had I gotten *that* wet?—center. "You're quite allowed to change your mind, no matter how far it's gotten."

"Of course I am," I murmured. "But I haven't."

He sighed. "Good. That's *very* good." The tip of him eased inside me.

I let out a noise. "You like the way things are going then?" I teased.

"Ice gods of the horizon, I wish I could scent you," he breathed.

"Oh," I said. "Well, all right."

"No. Not with…" His eyes rolled back in his head. He was pushing into me deeper now and he panted. "With Rehke."

I groaned. He felt good there. He was big and thick and he filled me everywhere, and I liked it. And I didn't want to think about Rehke, not in *this* moment.

So I snapped my hips up, engulfing Darce, taking his girth and his length, and he pierced me deep inside, and he let out a sound like a sob, and our mouths twined together as he thrust shallowly against me, seemingly instinctively, and I gasped against his lips until he pulled away.

He was out of breath, swallowing, and we were connected, completely connected. He turned his attention entirely to our joined pelvises, and that was when I remembered the little curved protuberances that the furrne men all had—the folioles.

He went to work on them, arranging them, tucking one around one side of my labia and one around the other and the third, the middle one… right *there*. I was slippery and slick there—from my own wetness, from his tongue, and the foliole slithered around against me, rubbing me in a *very* nice way.

I shuddered again.

"Good?" he breathed.

I couldn't make words. I moaned.

He kissed me again. "You feel…"

I moaned again.

"Like you were *made* to take me. The way you cling to me. You're so, so…" He groaned.

I undulated my hips.

He rose to meet me.

And then everything went white, and I was thrust back out over the icy horizon of goodness again, but it was twice as intense, because he was all the way inside me, he was joined to me, and he was rubbing me everywhere. His folioles slid against me as we thrust together, and his long, thick girth rubbed me inside, and I felt as though my pleasure center was trapped between both parts of him, squeezed pleasantly, and stimulated from all sides. I could also feel the other folioles, the ones outside my labia, and they seemed to be rubbing me too, helping out, nudging me off into the stratosphere.

I made garbled noises, and I wanted to kiss him, but I couldn't, because I felt as if I was coming apart and falling into pieces.

His tongue was at my throat and then on my breasts again.

That was too much.

I swelled up, like water under a crust of ice, and I shattered, ice shards everywhere, the gush of goodness beneath flowing through me, making me clench in an ecstasy of twitching squeezes, my body tightening around him in perfect, lovely spasms.

He let out a sigh of satisfaction, breathing into my skin. "Very good, Elizabeth. Just like that for me. *So* good."

My climax surged at his words, hitting another peak—even *better*—something I'd never done before.

Then it ebbed out, and his thrusts went erratic and quicker for a brief span of moments until he finished too, inside me, and I felt his body spasming too, like a reverberation of my own pleasure.

I wanted to melt into the bed.

I threw out my arms, letting out a soft, low groan.

He rained soft kisses over my body, kissing stray freckles here and there. "So, that wasn't a problem at all, Elizabeth. You came very easily for me."

I let out a helpless giggle. "You're such a cocky jerk sometimes, Darce."

"That's not translating." He was still kissing me. "I can only assume it's some kind of Earth compliment."

I laughed harder, and he was still inside me, and apparently my laughter did something to him, because he let out something like a growl and drove his hips into mine, pinning me to the bed, and my laughter faded into a gasp and I looked up at him, affected and overwhelmed.

This man…

"Apologies," he said darkly. "You… that movement…"

"Oops," I said.

He shook his head at me, a slow smile stealing across his face.

We just looked at each other.

And then we were kissing again, and I wrapped my thighs around him, and whispered, "Stay there. I want you to stay inside me."

"I don't ever want to leave," he murmured.

"Don't," I said, and then I yawned.

"Are you going to fall asleep, Elizabeth?" He was amused. "You know, amongst my species, it's usually the man who—"

"No, my species too," I said, tightening my thighs against him.

"We can't fall asleep like this."

"Can't we?"

"I'll crush you."

I let out a delighted laugh. "Mmm, you're not crushing me now."

"Yes, I'm holding myself up off of you so that I don't."

"Oh." I grinned at him. "So, all of your muscles are tense, and you're just exerting massive amounts of effort constantly, all for my enjoyment?"

"I don't know about massive amounts." He laughed. "So, you're enjoying this?"

"Nope, it's horrible, Darce. The worst night of my life."

He laughed again, a deep rolling laugh, and I'd never heard him laugh like that.

I smoothed my hands over his shoulders, basking in this feeling, whatever it was, because I liked it.

"Besides, we're supposed to talk," he said.

"Talk?" I might have almost whined this.

"You remember. You said we'd do this first, and that we'd talk afterwards."

"I don't want to talk," I said. Talking would mean delving into why this didn't make any sense, and possibly discussing Rehke, who… I shoved it all aside and yawned again. "Sleep first. Talk when we wake up."

He grunted. "I shouldn't let you convince me of that, but…" He yawned too. He gently began to extract himself, pulling his body out of mine, moving past my locked thighs like they were nothing.

"No," I said. "Stay."

"How about this?" he breathed, kissing my neck, "I'll be happy to be back here any time you ask. Over and over and—" He extracted himself. "Over." Another kiss.

I sighed.

He rolled off of me and pulled me into his arms.

I burrowed into him.

He engulfed me. He was huge and warm and solid and soft.

I hummed in happiness and satisfaction. I yawned.

"Elizabeth?"

"Hmm?"

"You're falling asleep?"

I sighed again and hummed once more.

He let out a chuckle.

Time passed, and I drifted.

I heard him whisper my name again, but I couldn't summon the energy to respond.

He let out a low groan. "Ice gods," he breathed, to himself, not to me, not really. "It's going to kill me to share you."

SIXTEEN

My bracelet woke me, and I sat up immediately.

Next to me, Elizabeth stirred.

Ice gods, she was here, in my blanic bed, naked and perfect and…

I snatched up the bracelet and kissed her bare shoulder. "Sleep, sweet one," I murmured, covering her with blankets as I eased out of the bed.

I went into the outer chamber of my bedchamber and pulled up the bracelet. Quickly, I scanned the frantic message I'd just received, fuming. This wasn't good.

Ice gods of the horizon!

I needed —

Well, handily enough, I'd taken my shirt off out here. I snatched it up and shrugged into it, even as I worked on sending out a query through the bracelet.

A holoprojection of a Toth faax appeared out of my bracelet, just his head and shoulders. Only my head and shoulders would be visible as well, so he'd never know I wasn't wearing pants. "You're the Prince of Plembe?" he said.

Wasn't the word we used, but I wasn't going to quibble. Close enough. "Certainly am," I said cheerily. Did I look as if I'd just gotten out of bed? Did I look as

"

if I'd just shared furs? Ice gods! "I understand that there's some push back to my ship."

"Looks like a military ship."

"We sent a manifest," I said. "Not a military ship at all. Those are the most talented entertainers on my planet. I sent them as a gift of goodwill to the Toth."

He blinked at me.

"There are jugglers." I let out a laugh that I hoped didn't sound too artificial.

"Why would you give us a gift? Why do you think you need to curry our favor?"

I shrugged. "I don't suppose I *do* need to, do I? The fact that other planets in the galaxy have had their representation in the galactic senate taken over by the Toth, I'm sure that's nothing we'd need to worry about here, not Plembe." I gave him a wide grin. "After all, we on this planet are such good friends of the Toth." *Buy it, you gratts, buy it,* I thought at him, calling him a Toth insult in my head.

He considered this. "Jugglers?"

"Also fire swallowers, tumblers, flying trapeze artists, singers, and a woman who can do amazing things with colored flags. You've never seen anything like it, I swear to you." I grinned again. "Enjoy. Remember us. Remember we're friends."

He inclined his head. "All right. I'll let them through. Sorry about the confusion."

"Not a problem," I said. "Can't be too careful these gesuns, after all." Gesun was how the Toth measured pleiccs on their planet, Geheri.

"No, you can't," he said.

We spoke briefly before he terminated the transmission and I got back in touch with Rehke to make sure that they'd been given access to the space station.

He confirmed that they had.

Then I didn't hear anything else, but I was antsy. I couldn't go back to sleep, and I didn't want to wake Elizabeth if I tossed and turned in bed with her, so I found some clothes, dressed hurriedly, and left the room. Just before I did, however, I opened a drawer and found one of my old bracelets. I wiped it and set it out on the table next to the bed. Elizabeth wanted a bracelet, and I wanted her to have one. I'd get her set up on it when we woke for the pleicc. Then I went downstairs to my study where I could track the ship and see its position, hopefully determine something from that while this was all going on.

I needed to think about that anyway, not whatever I'd done before going to sleep.

Not the intoxicating reality of Elizabeth's body, so much more lovely than I'd ever possibly imagined. I adored everything about her. How small she was, how soft, the noises she made when I pleased her, the way her smooth skin felt under my tongue, her wet and warm—

No.

Not thinking about that. About her. About her in my *bed* and *naked*.

I waited, watching, and the ship seemed to be docked at the station for far too long. Then a tracking device flared to life on the *other* ship, the Toth ship, the one full of women, and I watched as it went through its paces and detached from the station.

I watched as both ships left, both ships free and on a course for Plembe.

My heart in my throat, I sent a query to Rehke.

He responded with a query for video, and I accepted

and he appeared in my bracelet head and shoulders visible just like the Toth had. He was jubilant. "Oh, they never knew what hit them, Darce."

"It went all right, then?"

"Perfectly," he said. "I have to say I was worried when we couldn't get through, but whatever you said must have worked."

"I just pushed the ruse from the manifest," I said. "But I guess he believed it coming from me." And now he was dead, I supposed, since that was the plan, to massacre all the Toth on that station.

"It took you a while to answer."

"Well, it's the middle of the neicch."

"You're sleeping?" He chuckled.

I swallowed, shame flooding me. "Well... I'm not now. Couldn't sleep now."

"But you could before?"

I couldn't meet his gaze.

"Darce? You all right?"

"Maybe we should wrap this up," I muttered. "You're busy—"

"I'm the opposite of busy. We did it all. We'll be planetside soon enough. You're being strange."

"I shared furs with Elizabeth." It came out of my mouth before I could stop it. It shouldn't have. I didn't need to tell him that and not over bracelets and there was no reason to say it. "It just... happened." I sounded like Blenge. "But she specifically said that she would accept us both as suitors, so you'll have your—" I choked. "Turn."

His features were frozen.

I felt wretched.

"How many hihors ago was it that you were arguing until you were hoarse that I needed to stay out of harm's way for her sake?" he said in a low, lethal voice.

"No, I know that."

"You were convinced she didn't want you," he said. "Of course, I knew she did. I knew it. I could see it all over both of you, but she seemed to spew such venom about you, and I should have realized that was *part* of it—"

"Venom?"

He laughed harshly. "Go to the icy craggy depths, Darce." He snapped off the transmission.

I shut my eyes. Well. That hadn't gone well. I opened my eyes again. I supposed I should rejoin Elizabeth. We did have things to speak of, after all.

Pleicc was dawning, low and blue-green on the horizon, making the icy mountains in the distance glitter like jewels.

I made my way back to my bedchamber.

It was empty.

* * *

elizabeth

I woke up and Darce wasn't there, but I was not alone.

I scrambled backwards on the bed, pulling the blankets with me, covering myself, and I gaped at Her Splendor Catte. "Elizabeth Bennet," she said, spitting out my name as if it offended her.

"Y-your Splendor," I breathed. "Perhaps you could give me a minute to get dressed. If you wouldn't mind waiting—"

"You ought to know that I am not one to be trifled with. You'd think you would have realized that, considering I hold the high seat of this planet. And yet, here I find you, in my nephew's bed. What am I to make of that?"

"That it's none of your concern?"

She bared her teeth at me. "I won't have a half-breed on the high seat."

I blinked at her.

"He spent in you, I suppose. You carry his seed even now?"

I put my hand to my abdomen, through the blankets. Why had I not *thought* about that?

"If a child quickens within you, you will claim it is someone else's and not my nephew's. I will not allow our bloodline to be sullied and muddied—"

"Well, how else is your bloodline even going to survive?" I demanded.

"When I first heard of the illness, I had my daughter undergo a procedure that extracted several of her ovum, which have been kept in stasis, perfectly preserved, for my nephew's—"

"Wait, your daughter was Darce's cousin."

"I'm aware of that. The bloodline will be very pure."

"But it'll be incestuous and prone to mutation."

"That's not really true, not unless it happens over and over through numerous generations. One generation of incest is nothing."

I blinked.

"At any rate, you will cease all contact with my nephew, and you will not allow him to attempt to get you with child again, and—"

"Even if you had one more baby of your species," I said. "One more pure blood furrne, who are you going to mate *that* child with? The bloodline's getting muddied one way or the other, and you're *insane*."

"You will get *out* of this palace," she snapped.

Note to self, calling the queen of a planet insane? Not a great plan.

"I will keep you away from him," she said.

"You can't do that," I said. "Not if he wants to be near me. Darce isn't going to let you bully him. And if he wants to have babies with me, then I'm certainly not going to stand in the way of that."

"Well," she said. "*I* will stand in the way." She swept out of the room.

I glared after her.

Two minutes later, an army of servants entered the room. They had clothing for me, and they tried to force me to dress until I sent them off and agreed to put the clothes on myself.

Once dressed, they escorted me—well, dragged me—out of the palace.

Out there, alone in the cold, with nothing except a fur coat, I was very glad I'd picked up the bracelet that Darce had left for me. I'd memorized the address of Colle's house, in case I ever got lost, and I managed to figure out how to type it into the holokeyboard on the bracelet.

I pushed a bunch of holoprojected little buttons, and one of them opened an audio channel. I recognized the voice of one of the servants at Colle's house. "Please, I'm stuck outside the palace. Send a tirecraft. Oh, it's Elizabeth."

Within fifteen minutes, a tirecraft appeared. Colle and Charlotte were both inside.

"Why did you spend the night at the palace?" said Charlotte.

I shrugged. "Just… fell asleep there. It was late."

She eyed me. "Of course you'd want the prince. This is your private fairy tale, right, Elizabeth? Well, when you continue to complain about him, which is all you've *ever* done, do not come crying to me, okay?"

"I'm glad everyone's so supportive of my relationship with Darce," I said sullenly.

Colle cleared his throat. "Did, um, Her Splendor see you?"

"Why do you think I got tossed out in the cold with no way home?" I said.

"Oh," said Charlotte, eyes wide. "I thought you and Darce immediately started bickering."

"No," I said. "He's probably looking for me, in fact. He and I have a lot of things to discuss."

"Right." She nodded. "Because when you went to him to get him to explain himself, you didn't talk at all?"

"He had better ideas of things to do with his tongue," I said.

Charlotte looked surprised, and then let out a snicker.

Colle's eyes widened. "If you please, Elizabeth, let's have some decorum."

"Sorry," I muttered.

"Well, furrne tongues are quite, er…" said Charlotte.

"Charlotte." A guttural warning from Colle that almost sounded… well… I supposed they were happy enough in that way, and I didn't want to know a thing about it.

"I do need to contact him," I said.

However, when we got back to Colle's house, there was a message from Jane.

Lydia had apparently gone missing, and she'd left a message that she'd gone with Wihke.

Wihke?

What was he even doing there?

But I couldn't speak to Jane in real time, since she didn't have a bracelet. Instead, I demanded that Colle arrange for me to go to her. I didn't know where she and Lydia were being kept. We'd exchanged messages, but that didn't mean I had the first idea of how to get to her.

Colle didn't want to reveal the location, but when he heard how angry Her Splendor was with me, he decided it might be better if I didn't reside under his roof anymore, and so he sent me off in a tirecraft.

I traveled over a long, winding road through an icy landscape until we came to another house, one quite similar to the mansion where Blenge had lived, except larger. Jane met me at the front door and we embraced.

I clung to her, holding onto her as tightly as I could. "I missed you. I missed you," I said over and over, and she said it back. Jane was like family to me. She was as close to me as a sister. I pulled back to look at her. "I have so much to tell you."

"I know. I saw you on the newsfeeds, all over the capital," she laughed. "You're famous, Liz."

Was I famous? "It's a lot," I said. "But you have to tell me what's happened here first. How does Wihke come into it?"

"I don't even know," said Jane. "I never saw him, but I wondered what was going on with Lydia. She kept missing meals and being secretive. I thought he liked *you*, Liz, but I guess if he couldn't have you, he was happy to move on to another one of us."

"He's a playboy," I said. "Lydia's welcome to him."

Jane shrugged. "Maybe that's exactly what she's always wanted."

"Truthfully, even someone like Lydia shouldn't have to put up with him. He, um, Jane, he..." I couldn't finish the sentence.

"He what?"

I told her about what Wihke had done to Gige instead, about how young she'd been, about how she'd died. I told her about the money and the inheritance and how he'd wanted Gige's money and how he was not a good man.

Jane shuddered. "Everything you say makes him sound worse."

"You never liked him."

"I wanted to like him for you," she said.

"He, uh, that night when he came into my room and he said he was going to come back for us?"

"What about that night?"

"Well, and the first time, too, he…" I bit down on my bottom lip. "He just sort of made things happen. I felt as if I was just along for the ride, like it was already… but he never really got my consent, you know? And that last night, he made me give him a hand job and afterwards I felt…"

"Liz." She hugged me. "Oh, Liz."

"Dirty somehow," I breathed.

"Liz, I'm so sorry."

I hunched up my shoulders. "He's not a good man, Jane. We have to do something. Even Lydia shouldn't have to put up with him. Do we have any idea where they are?"

"How would we?"

I held up my bracelet. "Well, maybe we can somehow figure something out on this."

"You got one!" She grinned. "How'd you manage that?"

"You know. I just went to bed with Darce."

Her jaw dropped. "Girl, you are holding out on me. Start at the beginning."

I grinned. "Jane, I really did miss you." And

Blenge… should I tell her what Darce did? I needed to make Darce fix that. I had *so much* unfinished business with him.

"I have been going out my mind with no one but Lydia here, let me tell you," she said.

We linked arms and went into one of the plush sitting rooms in the mansion.

I started at the beginning, and I told her everything.

SEVENTEEN

There were a number of things I should have been dealing with.

The most pressing was that the ship full of human women had docked and we had nowhere to put them at present. The women were being kept three or four to a cell, just like the way we'd found Elizabeth and the others, and we needed to get them out of there and into safe and comfortable lodgings, and I couldn't think about how to solve that problem.

It boggled my mind that I hadn't thought of it before, but here we were.

The other thing was Rehke.

He was basically the closest thing I had to a brother these pleiccs, unless you counted Wihke, which... obviously didn't count, no matter how soft I was on him. I needed to somehow make things right with Rehke.

I didn't know how.

Then there was the newsfeed media, my aunt, the entire planet, all of whom wanted to know what we'd done and how it would affect us.

Instead, however, I was only concerned with finding Elizabeth.

I managed to get some servants to admit to me that

they'd bundled her up and left her outside the palace in the freezing cold, and that infuriated me. They told me it was on the orders of my aunt, which meant that I could excuse the servants' behavior, but that I was going to have to deal with my aunt at some point.

No woman who I'd just made love to should be taken from my chambers and tossed out into the cold. That was unacceptable, and if my aunt ever did anything disrespectful to Elizabeth again—

But I'd have to wait to deal with that, because I couldn't find Elizabeth.

On the off chance she'd found her way home, I contacted Colle.

He told me that he'd sent her off with Jane.

At this point, I was accosted by people intent on finding somewhere for the human girls. I said to put them in the palace. Let my aunt deal with *that*. It wasn't as if there wasn't room.

And then, I headed off to find myself a tirecraft, but who should be out in the vehicle bay but Rehke.

"Been looking for you," he said. "Hiding from me?"

"She's at your house," I said. "Colle sent her to Jane."

"Elizabeth is?" he said. We'd sent Jane and Lydia to the Firne estate that was Rehke's family home for safekeeping.

"Let's go together," I said. "I'm sure it'll be an extraordinarily comfortable journey, both of us trapped in the back of a tirecraft with no one else."

He sighed. "Extraordinarily."

We didn't talk.

It was several hihors, but we mostly didn't look at each other.

I tried to apologize. "I should have had more self-control—"

"It's been just as long for me, Darce," he said. "I don't know if any of the men on this planet have a lot in the way of self-control currently."

"But I—"

"No," he said. "Let's not do this right now."

So, we didn't.

When we arrived, we were shown into a sitting room on the bottom floor, where Elizabeth and Jane were waiting for us, standing shoulder to shoulder, neither looking pleased.

I wanted to go to her and pull her into my arms and kiss her and hold her against me. I couldn't believe I'd been denied crawling back into bed with her after our neicch together.

But Rehke was right there, and she was obviously angry with me—she was almost always angry with me, though, wasn't she?—so I only looked at the floor and was silent.

"Rehke," said Elizabeth. "I have... you and I... we should..."

"Yes," said Rehke, "actually, I was hoping we could speak alone, Elizabeth, because I—"

"The thing is, we have to save Lydia from Wihke first," said Elizabeth.

I raised my gaze. "What?"

She began to explain.

I listened, grimacing. "This is all my fault."

"A lot of things are your fault," said Elizabeth. "For instance, everything between Blenge and Jane."

I cringed. "When I did that, I thought that the human women should be kept from the men who were rich and powerful. I was thinking of the planet."

"Well, you broke Jane's heart," said Elizabeth.

"Obviously, it was a mistake," I said. "Obviously, I'll fix it."

"*Can* you fix it?" She put her hands on her hips.

I shifted on my feet.

Rehke cleared his throat. "About Wihke?"

"Right," I said. "I should kill him."

"Yes," he said.

"It's only that he's…"

"Family," said Rehke. "And so many have already died."

"Yes," I muttered.

"He doesn't have to die," said Elizabeth. "Maybe castration? What do we think of that?"

"Jail," said Rehke. "After what he did to Gige."

"Well, she's not here to speak against him," I said. "Maybe if he forced himself on Lydia?"

Rehke cleared his throat. "What about you?"

"Me?" said Elizabeth. "Wihke and I never…"

"Really?" I couldn't believe how pleased I was to hear that. "But he said that thing about your—"

"Well, he made me touch him," said Elizabeth.

"Made you," I repeated darkly.

"Yeah, like touch his, you know, his—"

"I got it," I said in a strangled voice.

"You know where his haunts are," said Rehke in a low voice.

"I do."

In unison, we turned and stalked out of the room.

"Wait, you're just leaving us here?" called Elizabeth after us.

Rehke and I halted.

"If you're coming," I said, "let's go."

EIGHTEEN

I couldn't believe Wihke hadn't even been a little bit worried someone would try to find him, but he obviously hadn't. This boarding house in the capital city was a place he'd come often. It was the first place I thought to look for him.

We banged on the door of the room where he was staying and from inside. I yelled, "Wihke, open up."

From within he called back, "Thank the ice gods, Darce. Took you long enough."

"Let us in."

"How much do you want that human girl back, Darce? How much is she worth to the planet? How much is her *womb* worth?"

"*This* is your plan?" I said.

"We shouldn't have expected anything different," said Rehke.

"Forget it," I yelled back through the door. "Not another blanic credit for you, and —"

Abruptly, the door opened.

The first thing I saw was a blaster, pointing right at my face. But then I realized that it wasn't Wihke holding it, it was Lydia.

She lifted her chin, gesturing with the blaster.

"Erm, Lydia," I said, looking over her shoulder at the

bed, where Wihke was crouched, hands tied together. "We're here to rescue you."

"Don't need rescuing," said Lydia.

"Obviously not," said Rehke, raising an eyebrow. He looked her over, grinning widely.

"You," said Wihke to Rehke. "You're always trailing along behind Darce, aren't you?"

"Well, go on, then, Lydia," said Rehke. "Shoot him."

Lydia lowered the blaster. "Well, if I was going to do that, I would have already."

"Just as well," I said blandly. "I thought we said we weren't going to kill him."

Rehke held out his hand for Lydia's blaster. "In the leg or something."

I lifted a hand. "Brint. Definitely do that."

"Darce!" Wihke was horrified.

Lydia did not hand over the blaster. "He just used me. He promised me all kinds of things, and he lied. I hate him." Her face twisted. "I'm so st-stupid." She started to sob.

"Oh, hey, you're not stupid," said Rehke, taking the blaster, handing it to me, and draping an arm around Lydia.

I raised the blaster and sighted Wihke.

"Darce, really, this human woman is insane. You can't believe anything she says," Wihke said.

"Did you lie to her, tell her that you cared about her, and then try to hold her for ransom?" I said.

"Well, saying ransom makes it sound, I don't know, criminal." Wihke shrugged.

Lydia was sniffling. "Are you going to shoot him?"

"I'm not sure. I thought we were sending him to jail," I said.

"If we shoot him, probably not," said Rehke. "It

won't look good for us."

I thought that through. He was right. The heir to the high seat and the next in line shooting some man in the leg and then sending him to prison? I couldn't imagine that would be a good look for the government. Wihke's trial would become a spectacle. I sighed, setting the blaster aside. "All right. I won't shoot him."

"Thank goodness you've seen reason, Darce," said Wihke. "Now, let's talk about—"

I cut him off by seizing him by the collar of his shirt.

"Darce!" said Wihke.

I shoved him into the wall. "You hurt Elizabeth."

"Hurt?" said Wihke. "I don't think that's the word I'd use. Liz and I had a very nice time together, and she—"

I slammed him into the wall again. "She was new to this planet, all alone, frightened, and you *forced* her to pleasure you."

"I did *not*."

"You're saying she's lying?"

He bared his teeth at me. "Put me down, Darce."

I slammed my fist into his face.

He howled.

I cringed, wringing out my hand. I hadn't punched people particularly often in my life. I was always forgetting how much it hurt.

Wihke had his bound hands to his nose. It was bleeding.

Well, however much it hurt, it was worth it.

"I've got an idea," I said to Wihke, twisting my lips into something like a smile. "Not jail, not being shot, just exactly what he wants."

"What I want?" said Wihke. "Credits?"

"Getting off planet," I said. "Isn't that what you were

on about last time we spoke?"

"But I've seen the newsfeeds," said Wihke. "And if you send me off planet now, after what you just did, taking that ship of women, well, I hardly think that's going to ingratiate our species to the Toth. You can't send me out there, not now." His voice was rising, growing panicked.

I turned to Rehke. "What do you think?"

"I think it's perfect for a waste of air like him," said Rehke.

"No," said Wihke. "For the sake of the gods, I'm bleeding here, and if you ship me through the lectre field, it's worse than shooting me. Darce, you can't do this to me, not to *me*. After everything we've been through?"

I looked him over. "I've given you a lot of chances, Wihke. You… there comes a point in time when…"

Wihke's lower lip started to tremble. "You've never given me anything like a fair shake, Darce. You had everything, always everything, and I've had *nothing*."

"That excuse, my friend, is wearing thin," I said.

* * *

elizabeth

Lydia was wrapped in a blanket, and she'd been silent for a long time, too long. I'd never seen Lydia like this.

Jane, Charlotte, and I hovered, none of us certain of what to say. What had Wihke done to her? Was she all right?

On the other hand, maybe she was angry with us for taking her away from Wihke. Maybe she'd wanted to stay with him. Maybe she'd been happy.

The four of us were in the upstairs game room in Colle's house. Colle might have objected to all of us being there, but he wasn't around to object, because he'd been summoned to the palace by Her Splendor, who was in the middle of having a nervous breakdown about all the human women in the palace.

Darce and Rehke were off dealing with that too, and possibly with Wihke being tossed off the planet into space, since they'd apparently determined exile was the best punishment for him.

I didn't entirely understand what the rules were on this planet when it came to women and consent, but obviously there were consequences for such things here. However, I wasn't sure what I wanted the consequences to be toward Wihke. When they'd been talking about killing him, I'd felt uncomfortable with that. I didn't want to bring about anyone's death, no matter what they'd done. It just wasn't in me to want that.

And if he were exiled, I didn't know what the Toth were going to do to him, because they were obviously going to be angry with the furrne for stealing human women from them.

What had he done to Lydia? Did she wish he was dead?

Charlotte asked Lydia if she wanted anything to eat or drink. This was probably the fifth time that Charlotte had asked and Lydia had remained silent during all of it.

But suddenly Lydia started to talk. "I have an older sister on Earth," she said, out of nowhere.

We all sat down on a couch facing her, and nodded, waiting.

"She's prettier than me," said Lydia. "Well, she was. She still had some baby fat to lose when I got abducted, and, um, I don't know, maybe while she's still a little pudgy, I might be prettier than her? Not that it matters, which of us is prettier."

I didn't say anything, but I was pretty sure that mattered to Lydia a *lot*.

Lydia kept talking. "Anyway, she's married now. She didn't want to get married, but she accidentally got pregnant. The guy, he told her that she wouldn't be able to get pregnant because he's sterile or something, but he was apparently lying. She doesn't even like him. And she's young, too. So young. Too young to be stuck with that liar of a guy and a baby and everything else? I… I never wanted to be like her. Ever. I was going to go and make something of myself."

Right. As a Playmate, by taking off her clothes for money. But I didn't say that out loud either.

"And then, it turns out," said Lydia, "that I'm just as stupid as she is when it comes to men. Wihke said things to me, but he was lying. About everything." She huddled into her blanket. "He never wanted me, not really. He was just kidnapping me to hold me for ransom, and not even for me, for my *womb*." She screwed up her face. "It's like I don't matter at all, not to anyone, and all I wanted was… was… to be pretty or sexy or desirable or something, you know? I just wanted… I thought if people wanted me, that would mean I mattered."

"No," said Jane. "That's not what makes you matter, Lydia."

I put a hand on Jane's shoulder. "I know what you mean, Lydia, actually. I really do."

Jane shot me a disbelieving look.

I shrugged, trying to communicate to her that yes, Lydia was an idiot, but that it made sense to me.

"My sister?" said Lydia. "Before she got pregnant

and was forced to marry that guy, she mattered, and then, it was like she was invisible. Like she had disappeared. Like… no one wanted her. I'm just terrified of that happening to me. And Wihke, it was like he knew exactly what to say to me."

"Yeah," I said. "That's how he is all right."

"He didn't care about either of us, Liz," said Lydia.

"No, I know," I said. "He was simply out for himself.'

"But I'm out for *my*self," said Lydia. "So, how could I be taken in by him like that?"

Jane scoffed. "Seriously? You just admit that?"

"You know, everyone's out for themselves," said Lydia. "Some people lie to themselves about it. And at least I had a blaster and I knew how to use it, thanks to Denne."

"I am not lying to myself," said Jane, squaring her shoulders. "I'm not out for myself. That's the most messed up thing I've ever heard."

Charlotte let out a little noise.

"What?" said Jane.

"Um, I see the sense in taking care of yourself is all," said Charlotte.

"Well, there's taking care of yourself and then there's being *out* for yourself," said Jane. "One is self-preservation, one is selfishness, and Lydia is apparently just fine with being selfish."

"I'd rather be selfish than stupid," said Lydia. "Don't think I didn't see what happened with you and Blenge, after all."

Jane's face crumpled. "What's that supposed to mean?" Her voice was tight.

"Well, I *am* stupid, so don't worry," said Lydia. "Blenge used you for sex. Wihke used me for sex, and he tried to use me for money. If I would have wised up—"

"Hey," I said, "neither of you are stupid. Wihke was manipulative, and we didn't see it coming. And Blenge... well, it's not his fault."

"It's not?" said Jane. "Actually, earlier, when you were talking to Darce about fixing things because I had a broken heart, I was trying to talk, but you guys just talked over me. So, what did Darce do, exactly?"

"Darce lied to Blenge and said you were afraid of him."

"What?" said Jane. "How could Blenge have *believed* that?"

"I think Darce was in a position to be really convincing, because he had this idea that he should keep us away from rich men on the planet, because he thought that if the lower classes saw that the human women had all gone to the upper classes, there would be civil war or riots or something."

"Oh," said Jane, furrowing her brow. "I guess he does have to think about that sort of thing."

"Wait, that's not a good excuse," I said. "Darce should never have lied."

"Well, no," said Jane. "Did you know this before you went to bed with him?"

"Um..." I bit down on my lip.

Jane stood up, planting her hands on her hips.

"Sorry," I said. "It just... it sort of happened."

"I know how that goes, actually," said Jane, sighing.

"Yeah," said Lydia wistfully.

"Mmm, not me," said Charlotte. "It was all very deliberate on my part. Actually, he needed a good bit of convincing and he must have asked permission eighty times."

I groaned. "Ugh, don't put pictures in my head of Colle and you in bed."

Charlotte laughed. "Haven't I done that already with all the times I've explained things that happened in graphic detail?"

"Well, stop," I said.

There was a query beep from the ceiling. "Charlotte, it's Blane, comm access requested?"

"Accepted," sang out Charlotte. "What can I do for you, Blane?" Blane was a servant at the house.

"There's a man here to see Jane Gardiner," came Blane's voice. "It's Blenge of the clan Leye. Can I send him up?"

We all looked at each other, surprised.

"Well, speak of the devil, and the devil appears," breathed Jane.

"You want to see him?" said Charlotte.

Jane nodded.

"Blane, send him up," said Charlotte.

Moments later, Blenge was standing in the doorway of the room, gazing at Jane as if he'd never truly thought he'd lay eyes on her again.

"Guys?" said Jane, who was staring back at him. "Can you give us a moment?"

Lydia sighed heavily, lifting up her blankets. "Sure, fine. I'll get up in the middle of the aftermath of my ordeal so that you can talk to the man who abandoned you or whatever."

"Lydia." I glared at her.

"What?" said Lydia, making a face at me.

I yanked her out of the room.

The door shut behind us, leaving Lydia, Charlotte, and me in the hallway.

"You know, Lydia," I said, "if you really want to be

desired, I think you're in the right place for it. There's a whole planet full of men here looking for women, and you're allowed to have multiple suitors, and they're allowed to fight over you, so… I mean, maybe all your dreams have come true."

Lydia turned to me with a wondering look on her face. "Oh, Liz, that might be the nicest thing anyone's ever said to me."

I fought to keep from rolling my eyes. I just patted her shoulder instead. "Yeah, you're welcome."

"I'm really glad not to be stuck with Wihke," she said. "What if it had been like my sister and I'd been forced to marry him?" She shuddered.

"Wait…" I nodded at her belly. "You're not…?"

"Oh, I don't think so," she said, shaking her head. "Wihke had these sort of space age condom things. Apparently, there's a surplus on the planet right now, since no one's much up for birth control."

Another query beep. "Charlotte?"

"Yes, Blane?" said Charlotte.

"There's someone else here. Rehke of the clan Firne. For Elizabeth Bennet?"

"Oh," said Charlotte, raising her eyebrows at me.

Rehke, huh?

Okay, I wasn't looking forward to this conversation.

I arranged it so that we could talk in a sitting room downstairs, and he was waiting for me when I got there. I had almost begged off. I wanted to tell him that Jane needed me or that I wasn't feeling well or something.

But in the end, I guessed I'd rather get it over with.

He was standing at one of the windows, and when I came in, he turned to me.

"I, um, shared furs with Darce," I said as a greeting. I

blurted it out. Ugh, what was wrong with me?

"I know." He looked away, back out the window. "So, right to it, then? Well, why not?"

I stood near the door. "Sorry. I guess we could exchange pleasantries first. How are you? How's it going at the palace?"

"We've got most of the new girls settled in rooms and we've been explaining to them what's happening and getting translators to them, and bracelets as well. Darce seemed to think that was important. He's getting them all loaded with the translation programs so that the women can read the text on the networks."

"Oh, I'd like a translation program."

"Here, I can download that for you." He turned again, holding out his hand.

I hesitated. Then I undid my bracelet and crossed to him, holding it out. "Listen, Rehke, I know that on your planet, that women are allowed to have more than one suitor, and I might have even said that I would accept you, but…" I swallowed. "The thing is, on my planet, once a woman goes to bed—shares furs—with another man, it's not… it's just, to me, it feels—"

"I understand." He gave me a small smile, taking the bracelet.

"How could you?"

"I've always thought it was barbaric, that custom," he said. "And oftentimes, it only causes pain. Women have usually already made their choices and then they feel obligated to get under furs with other men, and it's painful for everyone. I wouldn't demand that of you. I don't need that. I don't even *want* that." He turned his attention to the bracelet, pulling up a holoprojection and manipulating it with his fingers.

"Barbaric," I repeated.

"It's that not translating? What about… uncivilized?"

"No, I understood it, I… guess I just thought it was odd you'd say it that way."

"It's a remnant of a time before, when we were a primitive planet," he said. "I'm not saying there aren't women who don't enjoy the, er, freedom, and in that case, I think everyone wins, because there are a number of men who are quite eager and willing to share their furs with as many women as will have them." He laughed.

I laughed too. "I guess I can see that."

"So, perhaps it doesn't need to be abolished, not always." He shrugged. He handed the bracelet back. "There."

I blinked in surprise, because I realized that the projection was now in English. I gasped in delight, reading through a list of headlines from the newsfeeds, ones about the ball, about the ship full of women, all of it. "Thank you, Rehke, it's wonderful." I moved my hand and the projection went away. I was going to have to figure out these gestures, how to make the projection go away like that.

"Of course," he said. He smiled at me, a wistful sort of smile.

"Oh, Rehke," I breathed, sighing. "I don't know why, really. You make much more sense than him. I meant what I said about all the things that are right about you and the things that are wrong about him. It's me, I think. There's something wrong with me for wanting him anyway. And I shouldn't, because he still hasn't made amends in a number of ways, and yet…"

"Well, he's the heir to the high seat," said Rehke, shrugging, his grin widening.

"Rehke, that's… that makes him a worse choice. His duty to the planet will always be competing with affection for me—"

"I think I can safely say he puts you above the planet," said Rehke.

"No, he doesn't!" I was horrified at that thought and secretly thrilled.

"He's my best friend," said Rehke, shrugging at me. "He's my cousin. He's like a brother to me. I'm just very glad I never did anything with you, never once. I sort of knew to hold back, I think. I wanted… but it's better this way, don't you think?"

"I only…" I wanted to touch him, but I thought that would be a terrible idea. "What about you? What happens to you now? You should have someone. You're so wonderful, and I want you to be happy."

"Well, I hear there's a palace of human girls all waiting to meet someone fun." He waggled his eyebrows.

I laughed again.

Then it was quiet.

I fiddled with my bracelet, and the holoprojection popped up again, and it startled me, and I shrieked. Then I fumbled at it, trying to get it to go back, and Rehke reached over and helped me.

"Thank you."

His fingers lingered near my wrist.

We looked at each other.

His face twisted. He pulled his hand back. "I should go."

"Oh? Did you accomplish whatever it was that you came to tell me? Why did you come?"

"I have the answers to all my questions," he said softly.

My heart squeezed painfully. So, he'd come here with hope, then, and I'd squelched it. He was taking it well, there was that, but I felt horrible. "I'm sorry," I breathed.

"Don't," he said. "That's not going to make it any easier."

"Maybe it shouldn't be easy," I said. "Maybe if you're going to hurt, I should hurt just a little bit."

"Why? What tremendously awful thing have you done lately?" He was gentle.

"But you… I led you to believe… I said things…"

"Elizabeth."

"And I even *felt* things, but then… he…"

"It's all right."

"It's not," I said.

He considered. "It's not," he agreed finally. "Obviously, I wish it was different. I wish you picked me. I wish you'd never touched him. I wish we were kissing right now. I wish…" He let out a breath, squaring his shoulders. "But there's no point in any of those wishes, not truly. And it's as I said, I never dreamed of getting to marry someone I chose or that I loved. I always thought it was going to be some awful competition between me and five other nobles over some spoiled heiress who wasn't the least bit interested in me, and there *is* an entire palace of human women, after all, and…" He reached out and seized my hand. "He got those girls for you, Elizabeth, but it's going to be good for all of us, I think." He brought my hand to his mouth and he kissed the tip of my thumb. Then he let go of me.

I swallowed. "I just…"

He shook his head. "I'm leaving now. There's nothing else to say."

I tried to summon something anyway, but all that rose was a lump in my throat and a feeling of sadness and guilt.

He turned without another word and walked out of the room.

I watched him go, and then I collapsed onto a couch. That was so much worse than I had even imagined it would be.

NINETEEN

"So, then Darce made him question everything," said Jane. "Blenge was horrified to think that he might have hurt me or done things to me against my will. He's been in a deep depression since we were parted. He hated himself for what he thought he put me through. And I suppose I did go through something bad, but it was only missing him and thinking he didn't care about me. And all the time, we could have been together."

"So, what brought him here?" I said.

"Darce sent him a message on his bracelet, apologizing," said Jane.

"Oh, was there groveling?" I said.

"He didn't tell me what Darce said," Jane laughed.

"Hopefully, he groveled," I said. "I'm still waiting around for my groveling, which he hasn't really done, has he?"

"No, and you're owed a good bit of groveling," Jane agreed.

"Anyway, so Blenge is your suitor?" I said.

"My one and only," said Jane. "And we're going to get married. Soon. Because once we're married, I can move into his house with him, and until then we just have to visit each other, and I want to spend every waking moment with him." She giggled.

"Oh, you have it bad," I said, grinning at her.

"I do, I do." She was beaming. "It's good. Liz, everything… the abduction… the breeding program… we've been through hell. I'm due for something good."

"Overdue," I said.

My bracelet beeped.

I lifted it, squinting. I poked a little holoprojection that had popped up and a big message of words popped up. *Rehke told me he put the translation program on your bracelet. Can you read this?*

"It's from Darce," I said to Jane. I poked around a little more until I figured out how to send a response.

I can read it.

Brint. I'd like to talk, if you don't mind. Are you busy?

I could make time.

I'll send a tirecraft.

I smiled at Jane. "Here comes my groveling, I think."

But after I was taken in the tirecraft to the palace and shown to Darce's bedroom, I was there alone for some time. I had a platter of cheeses and fruits, and I sat and ate them, getting more and more annoyed as time passed.

Eventually, he appeared, looking harried and exhausted. "I'm going to murder my aunt," he greeted me.

"It's her fault that you've kept me waiting?" I said. "Well, I already have a list of grievances against her. I suppose I can just add that to the list."

"It's… everything." He clawed at the collar to his shirt, opening it up to free his neck, showing me some of the dark hair on his chest. "All these women, getting rid of Wihke, the threats from the Toth."

"Threats?"

"They can't get to us. The threats are empty." He came over and sat next to me and ate a small tiny fruit—like a pink grape almost? They were delicious, and I didn't know what they were called. "I'm just glad to be here with you."

I smiled. "Yes, do you have anything to say to me?"

He raised his eyebrows. "Definitely, lots of things. I can't remember any of them at the moment, because I'm still trying to worry about whether we have enough rooms for the human girls, but give me a moment, I'm sure it will all come back."

I waited.

"Oh, you told Rehke you didn't want him to be your suitor? You chose me?" He sounded surprised.

"You didn't want me to do that?"

"No, it was the best news I'd heard all pleicc, but… I just… I thought you…" He gave me a lopsided grin. "Does that mean you're… mine?"

I folded my arms over my chest. "I think we're skipping a lot of steps here."

He furrowed his brow. "You're annoyed with me. Well, that's actually typical, isn't it? I bet you're also not going to tell me *why* you're annoyed either, and the fact that I won't be able to guess it properly will make you even more annoyed." He sighed heavily.

"You are unbelievable," I snapped. "What is wrong with you?"

He ate another pink grape.

"You know that we were interrupted and that we have things to talk about," I said.

"Well, Blenge… he told me all is well with him and Jane, so that's all taken care of. What else did we need to talk about?"

"Taken care of? Aren't you sorry?"

"I already indicated how sorry I was."

"Did you." I glared at him.

"I think so," he said. He looked me over. "Was that not, um, satisfactory for you?"

"I'm going to require a real apology, Darce," I said. "And a grand gesture wouldn't go awry."

"Grand gesture? I defied the evil alien overlords to bring women to this planet to save you."

I blinked at him. "Oh?"

"I figured out the translation and got you books."

"That was nice. I did appreciate that."

"I exiled the man who sexually assaulted you, even though I considered him sort of like my brother and had let him get by with all manner of awful things up to this point, especially in regards to the death of my own sister, but you, when it was *you*, that's when I took action."

"Well, that's… I mean…" I shrugged. "I mean, that's not terrible that you did that."

"And that's not even to mention the fact that I've gone against my aunt, the holder of the high seat, and flown in the face of all tradition to marry you."

"We're getting married? Were you going to ask me?"

"Elizabeth, would you like to marry me, live in a palace, and help me rule a planet?"

I giggled. "I don't know, are you ever going to apologize?"

He laughed. "*That's* what you want."

"I think I'm owed an apology."

"*Another* apology."

"Oh, Darce, when have you apologized?"

"I think the word 'apologies' comes out of my mouth numerous times every time we interact," he said.

I scoffed. "Not this time, though."

He smirked. He ate another pink grape. "You know, I might be more inclined to issue this apology you want so badly if you were… less clothed."

My jaw dropped. "You did not just say that."

He chewed on the grape and gave me a positively sinful look.

"You're a bit of an entitled, arrogant asshole, aren't you, Darce?"

"Entitled," he repeated. "That translates. Are you insulting me?"

I got up from my chair and began parting the eazclasp of my shirt, yanking it apart. "Oh, who would dare to insult the high and mighty Darce, heir to the high seat of the planet? Certainly not me."

"Right," he said. "You're going to make me suffer, I see." He gazed at the skin I was baring to him.

"That's exactly what I had in mind." I pulled my shirt off and hurled it at him.

It hit him in the face and slithered down into his lap. His expression gentled and he openly stared at me. "Won't you just agree to marry me, for the sake of the gods?"

"No," I said. I pointed at him. "Now you. Your shirt."

He raised his eyebrows. "Is this part of the suffering?"

"You could end it if you just apologized."

"Mmm. Ending it…" He chuckled softly. He pulled off his shirt and bared all of his beautiful, rippling muscular torso to me.

I sucked in a breath. "Y-you…"

He smiled.

I took off my supporter.

He let out a groan.

"Now," I said in a dark voice. "Apologize."

"I'm sorry," he said immediately. "Your breasts are *perfect*."

"Why are you sorry?"

"For *everything*." His voice was guttural. "Come over here."

"You can do better than that." I parted the eazclasp on my pants and pushed them down.

"Sorry for…" He swallowed. "Why am I supposed to be apologizing?"

"You are *astonishing*," I told him.

"How am I supposed to think when you're naked?"

"Take off your pants."

"Absolutely." He was out of them in seconds, and then he was coming across the room for me.

I danced backward, out of his grasp, waving a finger at him. "No, no, no. Until there's been a sufficient grovel, we can't—"

He caught me, one burly blue arm around my waist. He pulled my body against his.

I gasped.

He kissed me. "Marry me," he breathed against my mouth.

"Okay," I said, sighing.

He chuckled.

I wrapped my arms around him and my legs too, climbing him like a tree.

He held me under my backside, balancing me like I weighed nothing. "I really am sorry," he said to me in a whisper. "I never want to make you hurt, Elizabeth. I want to do the opposite of that. I only want to make you happy. And if I do make you feel… in any way… bad, you'll tell me, won't you?"

"You know I will." I kissed him.

"Actually, yes," he murmured against my lips. "You're not one for keeping your grievances to yourself, truthfully."

I giggled. "Take me to your bed."

"With pleasure."

Then I was laid out beneath him and he was over me. He put his forehead to my neck and rubbed it back and forth, making a little noise in his throat.

A thrill went through me. "Oh, you're scenting me, aren't you?"

"Definitely," he said in a gravelly voice. "Now, you're mine and anyone who gets close enough will know it."

I shut my eyes and hummed. "I like it," I decided.

He captured my lips with his own. "Elizabeth, I… you unmake me."

I sighed. "Okay, I really like *that*."

And then, for some time, he was kissing me and using his tongue on all my sensitive parts, and I was writhing against his ministrations.

Suddenly, I thought of something. I lifted my head. "Did you know that your aunt wanted to use your sperm and her daughter's eggs to make test tube babies?"

He lifted his head from my breasts. "What?"

"You're not going to do that, right?"

"Ane was my *cousin*," he said.

"Well, that's what I said, and then your aunt said that the bloodline would be pure, and that she wouldn't let me have your babies."

He crawled up over me. "How would she stop you?"

"Well, she wouldn't, but she said if I was already pregnant, I should lie about it."

His eyes widened. "Oh, right, you could be

pregnant, couldn't you?" He touched my belly.

I gasped.

"Would you…? How would you feel about that? I suppose we didn't really talk about it."

"Oh, it's definitely my duty to help repopulate the planet," I said. "I mean, I think you'll probably have to just be, you know, filling my womb with your seed, like, over and over and—"

He cut me off, kissing me fiercely.

I gasped against his mouth.

His fingers were suddenly between my legs, frantic and yet finding all the right spots, rubbing me with surprising skill.

I groaned. "How are you so *good* at that? We're not even the same species."

"That's an odd thing to say." His lips lingered close to mine. "Don't men on your planet prize themselves on pleasing their women?"

"Maybe some of them," I decided. "But you… you're so…"

His body against mine. "What am I?"

"Hard," I moaned.

He chuckled. "Well, that's accurate. I suppose if you're interested in having your, um, your womb filled with my…" His voice went gravelly. "*Seed*, that could be arranged."

I wriggled my pelvis against his. "Well, let's repopulate the planet, then, Darce. Not a moment to lose."

He chuckled softly. And then, he started moving his fingers on me again, working me into a frenzy. "You're not quite ready yet, I don't think," he breathed. "Patience, Elizabeth."

When he finally did slip into me, stretching me in the

sweetest of ways, I was like a live wire, sparking, ready to explode, and it barely took any time at all with his folioles moving against me before I was shooting off into space against him — around him.

He went slow as my climax overtook me and then faded out, and then he sped up again, and he made love to me until I felt another height of pleasure building, this one twice as intense.

It came for me like an avalanche of ice, tumbling down from the heights to bury me in sharp shards of sweet goodness, each one more powerful than the last. I took him with me, and he came also, his convulsions melding into mine, until I couldn't tell which of us was still coming, until I couldn't tell where he ended and I began.

I trembled in his arms when it was over, and he smoothed my hair away from my face and panted against me, kissing me — my jaw, my cheekbone, my temple.

"Elizabeth," he whispered. "Elizabeth."

I just held onto him, unable to make words, not even his name.

"I love you," he breathed.

"Yes," I said, and then I giggled. "I mean, me too. I mean —

His mouth was on mine, his tongue touching mine, sweetness bursting all around us like flowers coming to life.

TWENTY

I shouldn't have been surprised at how quickly I got her pregnant, I suppose. It certainly wasn't for lack of trying, but it was a bit mortifying that it had happened before I'd truly gotten around to marrying her, which was something I had to remedy immediately, in a bit of a hurry.

Truthfully, it was the sort of thing that never had to be worried about amongst our people because women always got pregnant after the third mooncross and all the marriages were typically conducted then and then the women went into season, and…

Well, things were different with humans.

Not bad different.

Not at all.

But it was surprising, the feeling of it. I hadn't anticipated what it would be. It was a surge of all sorts of confusing and contradictory sensations and emotions. The idea that I'd somehow altered her body, left something in her that was, well, growing in her, it was oddly gratifying in a sort of way I can't even describe. Really, sort of an embarrassing thing to admit, but it was powerful, too, and it made me want her even more. I felt overwhelmingly possessive and it only spurred me on to make sure the wedding happened more quickly — even if it was not the traditional time for weddings.

Traditions be taken to the icy, craggy depths, truly.

None of that mattered.

And it was very affecting how my feelings for her kept changing and intensifying to frightening degrees. It was honestly unfathomable, because I could have sworn that I already loved her more than I'd ever loved anyone, and then she'd move in such a way or look at me, and I would suddenly feel something so much *more*, and the feeling I'd had before seemed like nothing.

And then there was guilt. She developed sickness as the baby grew in her, and it was my fault she was even pregnant. I had caused this to happen. I had made her uncomfortable. And it was going to be worse. There was going to be this piece of me gestating in her and she was going to have to birth it, and we'd never... what if it didn't work well, humans giving birth to half-blooded furrnes? Ice gods! The blanic anxiety was unbearable.

All the while of course, I wanted to spare her whatever anxiety she must have been feeling, and I didn't want her to know that I was in abject terror about having done this to her.

Meanwhile, there were hundreds of other human women, and my aunt was in a bad mood — not least because of how quickly I'd impregnated Elizabeth and married her — and I was pulled in all sorts of directions.

Blenge and I hadn't spoken much for quite some time, but having wives who were so close helped bring us together, and Blenge had gotten Jane with child just as quickly as I had, so there was at least someone else going through it all, and we all spent a great deal of time together.

This necessitated a good bit of time spent with Carle, Blenge's sister, as well. I wish I could say that she took the fact that I had settled down with Elizabeth gracefully, but grace was not Carle's way. However, though it took her some time to accept it all, she eventually stopped being nasty, at least outwardly.

I could not say what it was for Carle to exist as a furrne women in those days, but I knew it must be difficult, and for her sake, we all gave *her* grace.

Colle and Charlotte announced their own pregnancy soon afterwards, and Elizabeth told me that Charlotte had been quite frightened for it to have taken so long. Wouldn't it have been something to come across the galaxy to a planet, prized for your womb, and then find yourself barren? But Charlotte was not, and indeed — as the years passed — she and Colle reproduced at a remarkable rate.

As for Lydia, she was in no hurry to settle down at all. Instead, she seemed interested in setting the record for the most suitors a woman could possibly have at once, and since there were not necessarily enough women to go around, no one seemed to mind. If Lydia was pleased and everyone else was pleased, I decided to keep out of it.

Of course, there was the fact that Rehke lost very little time in becoming one of her suitors. I thought he could do better, but he said that the image of her with that blaster was burned into his brain, fascinating, appealing, and ever so erotic.

Lydia was equal opportunity with her suitors, never demanding exclusivity from them. They were free to court other women while they courted her.

So, Rehke never gave her up, not exactly, but he had

other conquests. I kept waiting for him to settle down with someone else, someone worthy of him, personally, but he didn't. I couldn't say if that was because of Lydia or not.

I could say that he didn't seem upset about the circumstances. He would often return to a refrain about choice. He would say that he had never thought he'd have any choice when it came to women, that it would have all been decided for him. And this world, with its array of choices, well, he said he found that to be the most appealing thing of all.

If that were true, then he and Lydia were entirely well matched.

Some of the human women were settled with furrne men rather quickly. In spite of whatever I had thought, I didn't end up making any class restrictions on who could have one for a wife. Elizabeth told me that after everything the human women had been through, the last they needed was more things being decided for them. They had not chosen to be abducted by the Toth, and our rescue of them was just another abduction, truly. She said that they must have as many choices now as were possible, and I agreed with her. So, we let them decide themselves.

Lots of them didn't decide to get married or accept suitors at all, or at least not yet.

And that was fine, even though my aunt wasn't pleased by it.

The Toth were predictably annoyed, and they told us that if we ever came out from behind our lectre field, we'd be slaughtered. So, we didn't come out. And sadly, my predictions of Toth supremacy came to fruition rather quickly.

Soon enough, the Toth ruled the entire galaxy. Every

seat in the galactic senate was held by some Toth or other. And there were ship after ship of human women brought through the wormhole. Some with human men as well. They were used and abused in awful ways.

We watched all this from behind our lectre field, and we were safe. Isolated, yes, but safe.

Elizabeth's pregnancy passed without incident. We spent a lot of time trading books and having them translated. She soon learned to speak our language very well, even without the use of a translator. I was gratified to find that the Earth books were similar to ours in many ways. Obviously, there were many differences in culture and practices, but deep down, I thought, humans and furrne cared about the same things, and this was why my marriage to Elizabeth was so strong despite our differences.

Elizabeth gave birth to our daughter in what I thought was simply the most horrifically drawn-out labor and agonizing birth of all time. It was torture for me.

The midwife said it was mostly typical and even easy.

Neither Elizabeth nor I had any agreement with the midwife about the ease of it. But the fact was, my wife and daughter both came out of it healthy and neither were injured and it all… worked.

And our daughter?

She was…

It was that sensation again, of one's emotional capacity for love multiplying in one moment? I had never felt anything like it. I loved our sweet daughter, and my love for Elizabeth grew *again,* and I was utterly flattened by all of it.

Sometimes I wondered what would have happened

if we hadn't even gone on that Toth ship in the first place, if we'd never seen those women…

She had freckles.

My daughter.

We named her Genne, and she looked very furrne for the most part, but her skin was dappled like her mother's, and she was beautiful and smart and fierce and she would rule the planet one pleicc, and I was so grateful to be her father, to have been given the gift of watching this small, wonderful being grow up and take her place in the galaxy.

Some neicchs, we three sat together under the glass dome that allowed us to gaze up at the stars, and Genne sat on my lap and we told her about the planet where her mother had come from, and about the galaxy beyond, and she would ask questions and point with her little hands — she had thumbs like her mother — and I would wonder if anyone in the universe could ever feel as lucky and happy as I did.

Overhead and all around, the dark blanket of space swathed the planet of Plembe, broken only by the glittering brightness of the stars, and we were tucked away here, safe and together.

www.ingramcontent.com/pod-product-compliance
Lightning Source LLC
Chambersburg PA
CBHW071601150726
48000CB00004B/1559